KU-048-829

THIS BOOK BELONGS TO

Andrea

Pip and Herbert dine together

GREAT EXPECTATIONS

GREAT EXPECTATIONS

Charles Dickens

Geddes & Grosset

© This arrangement 1994 Geddes and Grosset Ltd,
David Dale House, New Lanark, Scotland.

All rights reserved. No part of this publication may be
reproduced, stored in a retrieval system, or transmitted,
in any form or by any means, electronic, mechanical,
photocopying, recording or otherwise without the
prior permission of the copyright holder.

ISBN 1 85534 557 9

Printed and bound in Slovenia

10 9 8 7 6 5 4 3 2

CONTENTS

LIST OF PLATES

1

Christmas Eve on the Marshes

Pip's real name was Philip Pirrip; but as he called himself Pip, when he was a little boy, he came to be called Pip by everybody else.

He lived in the marsh country, down by the river, and twenty miles from the sea; and on Christmas Eve—a cold afternoon towards evening—Pip had wandered into the churchyard, where his father and mother were buried.

Beyond the churchyard lay the marshes, and beyond the marshes lay the river; and such a fierce wind came rushing up from the sea that, suddenly feeling very much afraid at finding himself there alone, Pip began to cry.

"Hold your noise!" cried a terrible voice, as a man started up from among the graves at the side of the church porch. "Keep still, you little villain, or I'll cut your throat!"

A fearful man, all in coarse grey, with a great iron on his leg. A man with no hat, and with broken shoes and with an old rag tied round his head. A man that had been soaked in water, and smothered in mud, and lamed by stones; who limped and shivered, and glared and growled, and whose teeth chattered in his head, as he seized Pip by the chin.

"Tell us your name," said the man. "Quick!"

"Pip, sir," replied Pip, in terror.

"Once more," said the man, staring at him. "Give it mouth!"

"Pip. Pip, sir."

"Show us where you live," said the man. "Pint out the place."

Pip pointed to where the village lay—a mile or more from the church. And then the man turned him upside down, and emptied his pockets, in which there was nothing but a piece of bread; and placing Pip on a high tombstone, where the little fellow sat trembling, the man ate the bread ravenously.

"You young dog," said he, licking his lips, "what fat cheeks you ha' got! Darn me, if I couldn't eat 'em!"

Pip held tighter to the tombstone on which he had been placed—partly to keep himself on it; partly to keep himself from crying.

"Now look'ee here!" said the man. "Where's your mother?"

"There, sir," said Pip.

The man started, made a short run, and stopped, and looked over his shoulder.

"There, sir," Pip timidly explained, pointing to a tombstone. "'Also Georgiana, Wife of the above.' That's my mother."

"Oh!" said the man, coming back. "And who d'ye live with—supposing you're kindly let to live, which I ha'n't made up my mind about?"

"My sister, sir," answered the trembling Pip; "Mrs Joe Gargery—wife of Joe Gargery the blacksmith, sir."

"Blacksmith, eh?" said the man. And he looked down at his leg. Then he came closer to the tombstone, took Pip by both arms, and tilted him back as far as he could hold him.

"Now look'ee here," said the man; "you know what a file is?"

"Yes, sir."

"And you know what wittles is?"

"Yes, sir."

"You get me a file," and he tilted Pip over a little more. "And you get me wittles. You bring 'em both to me; or I'll have your heart and liver out." And he tilted Pip again.

Pip was dreadfully frightened, and so giddy, that he clung to him with both hands. Then the man held him by the arms, in an upright position, on the top of the stone, and went on in a fearful voice:—

"You bring me tomorrow morning early, that file and them wittles, at that old Battery over yonder. You do it, and you never dare to say a word concerning your having seen such a person as me; and you shall be let to live. You fail, and your heart and your liver shall be tore out, roasted, and ate. Now, I ain't alone, as you may think I am. There's a young man hid with me, that has a secret way of getting at a boy, and at his heart and at his liver. A boy may lock his door, may be warm in bed, may think himself comfortable and safe; but that young man will softly creep and creep his way to him, and tear him open. Now what do you say?"

Pip said he would get him the file, and what broken bits of food he could find, and would come to him at the Battery early in the morning.

The man then lifted him off the tombstone. "Now," said he, "you remember what you've undertook, and you remember that young man, and you get home!"

Then he hugged his shuddering body in both arms, and limped towards the low church wall, and got over it like a man whose legs are numbed and stiff; while Pip, looking all round for the horrible young man, ran home as fast as he could, without stopping.

Pip's sister, Mrs Joe Gargery, was a tall, bony, bad-tempered woman, with black hair and eyes; and she was more than twenty years older than Pip, whom, as she boasted to the neighbours, she had brought up "by hand".

Joe Gargery, her husband, a fair man with curls of flaxen hair on each side of his face, was a mild, good-natured, easy-going giant of a blacksmith, whose forge adjoined his wooden house.

When Pip came home from the churchyard, the forge was shut up, and Joe was sitting alone in the kitchen. And the moment Pip raised the latch of the door and peeped in, Joe said:

"Mrs Joe has been out a dozen times looking for you, Pip. And she's out now making it a baker's dozen. And what's worse, Pip, she's got Tickler with her."

At this dismal news, Pip twisted the only button on his waistcoat round and round, and looked sadly at the fire; for Tickler was a wax-ended piece of cane, worn smooth with whipping Pip.

"She sot down," said Joe, "and she got up, and she made a grab at Tickler, and she rampaged out. That's what she did, Pip."

"Has she been gone long, Joe?" said Pip.

"Well," said Joe, glancing at the Dutch clock, "she'd been on the rampage, this last spell, about five minutes. She's a-coming. Get, behind the door, old chap, and have the jack-towel betwixt you."

Pip took his advice. Mrs Joe, flinging the door wide open, and finding something behind it, immediately guessed the cause, and, applying Tickler to her heart's content, ended by throwing the boy at Joe. Joe, glad to get hold of the little fellow, passed him on into the chimney corner, and the blacksmith fenced him up there with his great leg.

"Where have you been, you young monkey?" said Mrs Joe, stamping her foot. "Tell me directly what you've been doing to wear me away with fright and worry, or I'd have you out of that corner, if you was fifty Pips, and he was five hundred Joes."

"I've only been to the churchyard," said Pip, crying and rubbing himself.

"Churchyard!" repeated Mrs Joe. "If it warn't for me, you'd have been to the churchyard long ago, and stayed there. You'll drive *me* to the churchyard betwixt you two, one of these days, and oh, a pr-r-recious pair you'd be without me!"

Then she began, to set the tea things, while Joe peeped down at Pip over his leg. Mrs Joe spread some butter on the loaf, and then, sawing off a very thick round, she cut the slice into two halves, of which Joe got one, and Pip the other.

Pip was hungry; but he dared not eat his slice. He felt that he must have something for his dreadful acquaintance of the churchyard, and for the still more dreadful young man; and he resolved to put his hunk of bread and butter down the leg of his trousers.

Joe and Pip were the best of friends, and in Joe's good-natured companionship with the little boy, it was their evening habit to compare the way they bit through their slices, by silently holding them up to each other's admiration, now and then.

Tonight, Joe several times invited Pip to enter upon their usual friendly competition; but Pip took no notice, and sat with his yellow mug of tea on one knee, and his untouched bread and butter on the other.

At last, in desperation, Pip took advantage of a moment when Joe's head was turned away, and got his bread and butter down his leg. Joe was evidently made uncomfortable by what he supposed to be Pip's loss of appetite, and took a thoughtful bite out of his slice—which he did not seem to enjoy—when suddenly his eye fell on Pip, and he saw that the bread and butter was gone.

"Pip, old chap!" said Joe, staring at him with the greatest concern. "You'll do yourself a mischief. It'll stick somewhere. You can't have chawed it, Pip?"

"What's the matter?" said Mrs Joe, putting down her cup.

"If you can cough any trifle on it up, Pip," went on Joe, aghast, "I'd recommend you to do it. Manners is manners, but still your 'elth's your 'elth."

"What's the matter?" repeated Mrs Joe, more sharply than before.

"You know, Pip," said Joe solemnly, "you and me is always friends, and I'd be the last to tell upon you, any time. But such a—" he moved his chair and looked about the floor, and then again at Pip— "such an uncommon bolt as that!"

"Been bolting his food, has he?" cried Mrs Joe. And with that, she made a dive at Pip, and fished him up by the hair. "You come along and be dosed," said she. And as tar-water in those days was considered an excellent medicine—of which Mrs Joe always kept a supply—she poured half a pint of the nasty mixture down the boy's throat, holding his head under her arm, as a boot would be held in a boot-jack.

Poor Pip! The guilty knowledge that he was going to rob Mrs Joe, added to the necessity of always keeping one hand on his bread and butter, almost drove him out of his mind. But by-and-by he managed to slip away, and hid the bread and butter in his garret bedroom.

"Hark!" said Pip, as he sat later in the chimney corner. "Was that great guns, Joe?"

"Ah!" said Joe. "There's another convict off."

"What does that mean, Joe?" asked Pip.

"Escaped. Escaped," explained Mrs Joe, snappishly.

"There was a convict off last night," said Joe, "after sunset gun. And they fired warning of him. And now it appears they are firing warning of another."

"Who's firing?" asked Pip.

"Drat that boy," interposed Mrs Joe, frowning at Pip over her sewing. "What a questioner he is! Ask no questions, and you'll be told no lies."

At that, Joe opened his mouth very wide, and put it into the form of a word that looked to Pip like "sulks". But the little boy could make nothing of it.

"Mrs Joe," said he at last, " I should like to know—if you wouldn't much mind—where the firing comes from?"

"Bless the boy!" exclaimed Mrs Joe. "From the Hulks."

"Oh-h!" said Pip, looking at Joe. "Hulks! And, please," he added, "what's Hulks?"

"That's the way with this boy!" exclaimed Mrs Joe. "Answer him one question, and he'll ask you a dozen directly. Hulks are prison ships, right 'cross th' meshes."

"I wonder who's put into prison ships, and why they're put there?" said the little boy.

It was too much for Mrs Joe. She immediately rose. "I tell you what, young fellow," said she, "I didn't bring you up by hand to badger people's lives out. People are put in the Hulks because they murder, and because they rob and forge, and do all sorts of bad; and they always begin by asking questions. Now, you get along to bed!"

Pip was never allowed a candle to light him to bed and, as he went upstairs in the dark, he felt that the Hulks were very handy for him, and that he was clearly on his way there. He had begun by asking questions, and he was going to rob Mrs Joe.

He was in dreadful terror of the young man who wanted his heart and liver, and in dreadful terror of the man with the iron on his leg. He was afraid to sleep, even if he had been so inclined, for he knew that—at the first dawn of morning—he must rob the pantry. And if he slept at all that night, he dreamed that he was drifting down the river on a strong spring tide to the Hulks.

As soon as the grey light stole through his little window, Pip got up and went downstairs. He took some bread, some rind of cheese, and about half a jar of mincemeat, which he tied up in his pocket handkerchief with his last night's slice. Then he poured some brandy from a stone bottle into a glass bottle of his own, and filled up the brandy bottle from a jug in the kitchen cupboard. He also took a meat bone, and a beautiful, round,

"You young dog, what fat cheeks you ha' got!"

whole pork pie. There was a door in the kitchen leading into the forge. Unbolting that door, he got a file from among Joe's tools. Then he replaced the fastenings as he had found them, opened the door at which he had entered last night, shut it, and ran for the misty marshes.

2

A Chase in the King's Name

It was a rainy morning and very damp, and Pip's conscience pricked him so much, that he fancied the very cows, feeding on the marshes and staring hard at him, seemed to be saying, "Hulloa, young thief!"

Pip knew his way to the Battery pretty straight, for he had been down there on a Sunday with Joe; but, confused by the mist, he found he had gone too far to the right, and so had to make his way back along the riverside.

He had just crossed a ditch which he knew to be near the Battery, and had just scrambled up the mound beyond the ditch, when he saw the man sitting before him. His back was towards Pip, and he had his arms folded, and was nodding forward, heavy with sleep; and Pip, going on softly, touched him on the shoulder.

He instantly jumped up, and it was not the same man, *but another man!* And yet he, too, was dressed in coarse grey, and had a great iron on his leg, and was lame, and hoarse and cold; but he had not the same face, and wore a flat, broad-brimmed felt hat.

He swore an oath at Pip, made a hit at him, with a weak blow that did not touch him, and ran on into the mist.

"It's the young man," thought Pip—the young man that wanted his heart and liver. And running on in terror he got to the Battery at last, and there was the right man hugging himself, and limping to and fro, waiting for Pip.

He was frightfully cold, and his eyes looked so awfully hungry, that when Pip handed him the file he thought he was going to eat it.

"What's in the bottle, boy?" said he.

"Brandy," answered Pip.

The man put the liquor to his mouth; and he shivered so violently, that it was as much as he could do to keep the neck of the bottle between his teeth without biting it off. And then he began to gobble mincemeat, meat bone, bread, cheese, and pork pie all at once, staring distrustfully while he did so through the mist, and often stopping his jaws to listen. Some real or fancied sound now gave him a start and he said suddenly:

You're not a deceiving imp? You brought no one with you?"

"No, sir!" said Pip. "No."

"Nor giv' no one the office to follow you?"

"No!" said Pip again.

"Well," said he, "I believe you. You'd be but a fierce young hound, indeed, if, at your time of life, you could help to hunt a wretched warmint, hunted as near death as this poor, wretched warmint is!" Something clicked in his throat, as if he had works in him like a clock, and was going to strike. And he smeared his ragged sleeve over his eyes.

Pitying his desolation, and watching him as he gradually settled down upon the pie, Pip made bold to say, "I am glad you enjoy it."

"Thank'ee, my boy," said he. "I do."

"I'm afraid," said Pip timidly, after a silence, "you won't leave any of it for him."

"Any for him? Who's him?" said the man, stopping in his crunching of pie crust.

"The young man that you spoke of," said Pip. "That was hid with you."

"Oh, ah!" he returned with something like a gruff laugh. "Him. Yes, yes. *He* don't want no wittles."

"I thought he looked as if he did," said Pip.

The man stopped eating, and stared at Pip with the greatest surprise. "Looked! When?"

"Just now," replied Pip.

"Where?"

"Yonder," said Pip, pointing. "Over there, where I found him nodding asleep, and thought it was you."

The man seized Pip by the collar, and stared at him so hard that Pip went on, trembling, "Dressed like you, you know, only with a hat, and—and with an iron on his leg. Didn't you hear the guns last night?"

"Then there *was* firing," he muttered to himself. "But this man," he added suddenly to Pip, "did you notice anything in him?"

"He had a badly bruised face," said Pip.

"Not here?" exclaimed the man, striking his cheek with the flat of his hand.

"Yes, there," said Pip.

"Where is he?" cried the man, cramming what little food was

left in the breast of his grey jacket. "Show me the way he went. I'll pull him down like a bloodhound. Curse this iron on my sore leg! Give us hold of the file, boy." And going down on the rank, wet grass, he filed at his iron like a madman, taking no more notice of Pip.

"I must go home now, sir," said Pip timidly. But still the man took no notice; and Pip thought the best thing he could do was to slip off.

Pip fully expected to find a constable in the kitchen, waiting to take him up. But not only was there no constable there, but no discovery had yet been made of the robbery.

"And where ha' you been?" said Mrs Joe, who was getting the house ready for the Christmas festivities

"I've been listening to the carols," said Pip.

They were to have a superb dinner, consisting of a leg of pickled pork and greens, and a pair of roast, stuffed fowls. A handsome mince pie had been made yesterday morning (which accounted for the mincemeat not being missed), and the pudding was already on the boil.

But Pip was wretched under the weight of his wicked secret, and was seized with terror whenever Mrs Joe went near the pantry.

Mrs Joe put clean white curtains up, tacked a new flowered flounce across the wide chimney, and uncovered the little state parlour across the passage.

Mr Wopsle, the church clerk, was to dine with them, and Mr Hubble, the wheelwright, and Mrs Hubble; also Joe's uncle, Mr Pumblechook, who was a well-to-do corn chandler in the nearest town, and drove his own chaise cart.

Joe and Pip went to church, and when they got home, they found the table laid, Mrs Joe dressed, and the dinner nearly ready. The front door, too, was unlocked for the company to enter by, and everything was most splendid. And still not a word of the robbery.

Mr Wopsle arrived first, then Mr and Mrs Hubble, and last of all Uncle Pumblechook.

"Mrs Joe," said Uncle Pumblechook—a large, hard-breathing, middle-aged, slow man, with a mouth like a fish—"I have brought you, as the compliments of the season, a bottle of sherry wine, mum, and I have brought you, mum, a bottle of port wine."

"Oh, Un-cle Pum-ble-chook!" said Mrs Joe. "This is kind!"

"It's no more than your merits," retorted Uncle Pumblechook. "Boy," said he to Pip, as they sat down to dinner, "be grateful to them which brought you up by hand."

Mrs Hubble shook her head. "Why is it," she asked, "that the young are never grateful?"

"Naterally wicious," said Mr Hubble. While everybody else murmured, "True!"

Joe's way of comforting Pip at such times was to give him gravy; and he spooned into Pip's plate about half a pint.

Mr Wopsle praised the pork for being so plump and juicy. "And yet," put in Mr Pumblechook, "pork—when biled—is rich, too, ain't it?"

"Have a little brandy, uncle," said Mrs Joe.

It had come at last! Pip felt that he was lost. Mr Pumblechook would find the brandy weak, and he would say so. Pip held tight to the leg of the table under the cloth with both hands, and awaited his fate.

Mrs Joe went for the stone bottle, and returning with it, poured the brandy out. Mr Pumblechook took up the glass, looked at it through the light, and put it down. Pip couldn't keep his eyes off him.

Presently Mr Pumblechook took up the glass, smiled, threw his head back, and drank the brandy off. Instantly after, the company were seized with consternation, owing to his springing to his feet, and rushing out at the door. They then saw him, through the window, violently plunging and spitting, and making the most hideous faces.

Pip held on tight to the table, while Mrs Joe and Joe ran to Mr Pumblechook. Presently they brought him back, and he sank into his chair, gasping, "Tar!" Pip had filled up the brandy bottle from the tar-water jug!

"Tar!" cried Mrs Joe in amazement. "Why, how ever could tar come there?"

But Uncle Pumblechook, waving the subject away, asked imperiously for hot gin and water. Mrs Joe busied herself in getting the gin; and Pip became calm enough to release his grasp of the table.

The dinner proceeded, and presently Mrs Joe said, addressing the guests, "You must taste, to finish with, such a delicious present of Uncle Pumblechook's. It's a pie—a savoury pork pie."

The company murmured their compliments, while Mr Pumblechook said pompously, "Well, Mrs Joe, we'll do our best endeavours. Let us have a cut at this same pie."

Mrs Joe went out to get it. Pip heard Mr Hubble remark, that "a bit of savoury pork pie would lay atop of anything you could mention, and do no harm." And he heard Joe say, "You shall have some, Pip."

Pip was never sure whether he uttered a shrill yell of terror. He felt that he could bear no more, and that he must run away. He let go the leg of the table, and ran for his life.

But he ran no further than the house door, for there he ran head foremost into a party of soldiers with their muskets; one of whom held out a pair of handcuffs, saying to his comrades, "Here you are! Look sharp! Come on!"

The soldiers rang down the butt ends of their loaded muskets on the doorstep; and the dinner party rose from the table in confusion.

Mrs Joe, running back empty-handed from the pantry, began, "Gracious goodness me! What's gone with the pie?" And stopped short.

"Excuse me, ladies and gentlemen," said the sergeant, walking in with his hand on Pip's shoulder. "I am on a chase in the name of the King, and I want the blacksmith. We have had an accident with these"—holding out the handcuffs—"and I find the lock of one of 'em goes wrong. As they are wanted for immediate service, will you throw your eye over them, blacksmith?"

Joe threw his eyes over the handcuffs, and said the job could not be done without lighting the forge fire, which would take nearer two hours than one.

"Will it?" said the offhand sergeant. "Then will you set about it at once, blacksmith, as it's on his Majesty's service? And if my men can bear a hand anywhere, they'll make themselves useful." With that, he called to his men, who came trooping into the kitchen, and piled their arms in a corner.

"Convicts, sergeant?" asked Mr Wopsle, in a matter-of-fact way.

"Ay," returned the sergeant, "two. They're pretty well known to be out on the marshes still, and they won't try to get clear of 'em before dusk. Anybody here seen anything of such game?"

"No," everybody announced with confidence— except Pip. But nobody thought of Pip. And, beginning to see that the hand-cuffs were not for him, and that the soldiers had put the pie out of Mrs Joe's head, Pip began to collect his scattered senses.

Joe had got his coat and waistcoat off, and his leathern apron on, and passed into the forge. One of the soldiers opened its wooden shutters, another lighted the fire, another turned to at the bellows, the rest standing round the blaze which was soon roar-ing; and Joe began to hammer and clink, hammer and clink, while the others looked on.

At last Joe's job was done, and the ringing and the roaring ceased. And as Joe got his coat on again, he proposed that some of them should go down with the soldiers, and see what came of the hunt.

Mr Pumblechook and Mr Hubble declined, but Mr Wopsle said he would go, if Joe would. And Joe said he would take Pip, if Mrs Joe approved.

"If you bring the boy back with his head blown to bits by a musket," said Mrs Joe, "don't look to me to put it together again."

The sergeant then took a polite leave of the ladies. His men shouldered their muskets and fell in. Mr Wopsle, Joe and Pip received strict orders to keep in the rear, and to speak no word after they reached the marshes.

And as they all marched on, Pip whispered to Joe, "I hope, Joe, we shan't find 'em." And Joe whispered back to Pip, "I'd give a shilling, Pip, if they'd cut and run."

They held straight on to the churchyard, and here they were stopped by a signal from the sergeant; while two or three of his men searched among the graves. Then they struck out on the open marshes, and a bitter sleet came rattling against them; and Joe took Pip on his back.

And now, for the first time, Pip began to wonder, with great dread, if the convict would suppose that it was he who had brought the soldiers there—that he was indeed a deceiving imp, and had betrayed the convict.

But it was too late to think of that. There he was on Joe's back, and the soldiers were in front of them, moving on in the direction of the old Battery. Suddenly they all stopped, for there had reached them, on the wings of the wind, a long shout. It was repeated. And then there seemed to be two or more shouts raised together.

The sergeant ordered his men to make towards the sound "at the double," and away the soldiers ran. As they came nearer to the shouting, they heard, "Murder!" in one voice: while another voice called out, "Guard! This way for the runaway convicts!"

Then both voices seemed stifled in a struggle, and then they broke out again. And the soldiers ran faster than ever.

The sergeant ran in first; and Joe was not far behind. "Here are both men!" panted the sergeant, jumping down into a ditch. "Surrender, you two! What a pair of wild beasts! Come apart!"

Water was splashing, and mud was flying, and blows were being struck, when some more men went down into the ditch to help the sergeant; and they dragged out, separately, first Pip's convict, and then the other one. Pip knew them both directly.

"Mind," said Pip's convict, wiping blood from his face with his ragged sleeve, "*I* took him. *I* give him up to you. Mind that!"

"That'll do you small good," answered the sergeant. "Handcuffs, there!"

The other convict seemed to be bruised and torn all over, and had to lean upon a soldier to keep himself from falling. "Take notice, guard," he gasped, "he tried—he tried—to—murder me."

"Look'ee here," said Pip's convict to the sergeant. "Single-handed I got clear of the prison ship. I made a dash and I done it. I could ha' got clear of these marshes likewise—look at my leg; you won't find much iron on it—if I hadn't made discovery that *he* was here. Let *him* go free? Let *him* make a fool of me again? No, no, no!"

The other convict, who was evidently in extreme horror of his companion, repeated, "He—tried—to murder me."

"Enough of this wrangling," said the sergeant. "Light those torches."

As one of the soldiers, who carried a basket, went down on his knee to open it, Pip's convict looked round for the first time, and saw Pip. Pip, who had got off Joe's back, looked at him eagerly, and slightly moved his hands and shook his head, as if to say he was innocent of having brought the soldiers there. The convict gave him a strange look, and turned away.

The soldier with the basket soon got a light, and lighted three or four torches; while four soldiers, standing in a ring, fired twice into the air. Presently they saw other torches kindled on the marshes on the opposite side of the river. "All right," said the sergeant. "March!"

They had not gone far, when three cannon were fired ahead of the party. And the sergeant said to Pip's convict, "All right. You are expected on board. They know you are coming."

The two convicts were kept apart; and they were so lame and so tired, that two or three times the party had to halt while the convicts rested.

At last they came to a rough wooden hut and a landing place. There was a guard in the hut, and they challenged, and the sergeant answered; then the party went into the hut, where was a bright fire and a lamp; and soon the convict with the bruised face was put into the boat with his guard, to go on board the prison ship first.

Suddenly Pip's convict, who was staring thoughtfully into the fire, turned to the sergeant. "I want to say something," he said. "It may prevent some persons laying under suspicion alonger me. I took some wittles up at the village over yonder."

"You mean stole," said the sergeant.

"And I'll tell you where from," went on the convict "From the blacksmith's." But he never looked at Pip

"Hulloa!" said the sergeant, staring at Joe.

"Hulloa, Pip!" said Joe, staring at Pip.

"It was some broken wittles," went on the convict, "and a dram of liquor, and a pie."

"Have you happened to miss such a thing as a pie, blacksmith?" said the sergeant.

"My wife did, at the very moment when you came in," answered Joe.

"So," said the convict, turning his eyes on Joe, and never looking at Pip, "so you're the blacksmith, are you? Then I'm sorry to say, I've eat your pie."

"God knows you're welcome to it," answered Joe. "We don't know what you have done, but we wouldn't have you starved to death for it, poor miserable fellow-creatur.—Would us, Pip?"

The something that Pip had noticed before clicked in the convict's throat again, as if he had works in him like a clock; and he turned his back.

The boat had now returned, and Joe and Pip followed him and his guard to the rough landing place, and saw the convict put into the boat, which was rowed by a crew of convicts like himself.

Somebody in the boat growled, as if to dogs, "Give way, you!" And the boat rowed away.

By the light of the torches they saw the black Hulk lying out a little way from the mud of the shore, like a wicked Noah's Ark, barred and moored by massive rusty chains. They saw the boat go alongside, and they saw the convict taken up and disappear.

Then, the ends of the torches were flung hissing into the water and went out, as if it were all over with the convict; and Joe and Pip returned home.

3

A Wonderful Visit

When Pip should be old enough, he was to be apprenticed to Joe, and, for the present, he went to an evening school, kept by Mr Wopsle's great-aunt.

Mr Wopsle's great-aunt was always falling asleep and Pip would have learned very little, indeed, if it hadn't been for Biddy. Biddy was Mr Wopsle's great-aunt's granddaughter, and with her help, Pip gradually learned to read and write.

It was a full year after the hunt upon the marshes that Pip sat one evening in the chimney corner with his slate, writing, with great trouble, a letter to Joe. Joe sat beside him, and they were alone, and presently Pip put the slate into Joe's hand. And this is what Pip had written:

"MI DEER JO i OPE U R KRWITE WELL i OPE i SHAL SON B HABELL 4 2 TEEDGE U JO AN THEN WE SHORL B SO GLODD AN WEN i M PRENGTD 2 U JO WOT LARX AN BLEVE ME INF XN PIP."

"I say, Pip, old chap!" cried Joe, opening his blue eyes wide, "what a scholar you are! Ain't you?"

"I should like to be," said Pip.

"Why, here's a J," said Joe, "and a O equal to any-think! Here's a J and a O, Pip, and a J-O, Joe. You *are* a scholar, Pip."

"How do you spell Gargery, Joe?" asked Pip.

"I don't spell it at all," said Joe, rising to replenish the fire. "Here's the Dutch clock a-going to strike eight, and your sister's not come home yet! I hope Uncle Pumblechook's mare mayn't have set a forefoot on a piece of ice and gone down."

For Mrs Joe made a trip now and again to the town, on market days, with Uncle Pumblechook, and was out now on one of these expeditions.

Joe made the kitchen fire and swept the hearth, and then the two went to the door to listen for the chaise cart. And presently Joe said, "Here comes the mare, ringing like a peal of bells!"

The sound of the iron hoofs upon the hard, frosty ground was quite musical; and they got a chair out ready for Mrs Joe's alighting. Mrs Joe was soon landed, and Uncle Pumblechook was soon down, covering the mare with a cloth; and they all trooped into the snug kitchen.

"Now," said Mrs Joe, unwrapping herself in great excitement, "if this boy ain't grateful this night, he never will be! Miss Havisham wants this boy to go and play at her house. And of course, he's going. And he'd better play there," said Mrs Joe, shaking her head at Pip, "or I'll work him."

"Miss Havisham up town?" asked Joe.

"Is there any Miss Havisham down town?" snapped Mrs Joe.

Pip had heard of Miss Havisham up town as an immensely rich and grim lady, who lived in a large and dismal house, and who led a very retired life.

"Well, to be sure!" said Joe astounded. "I wonder how she come to know Pip!"

"Noodle!" cried Mrs Joe. "Who said she knew him? Couldn't she ask Uncle Pumblechook, if he knew of a boy to go and play there—Uncle Pumblechook, who's a tenant of hers, and who goes there quarterly to pay his rent? And couldn't Uncle Pumblechook mention this boy, that I have ever been a willing slave to?"

"Good!" cried Uncle Pumblechook. " Well put! Now, Joseph, you know the case."

"And Uncle Pumblechook," went on Mrs Joe, "has offered to take him into town tonight in his own chaise cart, and to keep him tonight, and to take him with his own hands to Miss Havisham's tomorrow morning. And Lor-a-mussy me!" cried Mrs Joe, throwing off her bonnet, "here I stand talking to mere mooncalfs, with Uncle Pumblechook waiting, and the boy grimed with dirt from the hair of his head to the sole of his foot!"

With that, she pounced on Pip, and his head was put under the tap of the water butt, and he was soaped, and kneaded, and towelled, and thumped, and put into clean linen, and was trussed up in his best suit, and was then delivered over to Mr Pumblechook, who said solemnly:

"Boy, be ever grateful to all friends, but especially unto them which brought you up by hand!"

"Goodbye, Joe!" said Pip.

"God bless you, Pip, old chap," said Joe.

Pip had never parted from Joe before; and what with his feelings, and what with soapsuds, Pip could at first see no stars from the chaise cart. But they twinkled out one by one, and Pip won-

His head was put under the tap.

dered why on earth he was going to play at Miss Havisham's, and what on earth he was expected to play at.

He slept that night at Mr Pumblechook's shop in the High Street of the market town; and at eight next morning he and Mr Pumblechook breakfasted in the parlour behind the shop.

Mr Pumblechook's conversation consisted of nothing but arithmetic, and he said pompously, "Seven times nine, boy?" And began a running sum that lasted all through the breakfast. "Seven?" "And four?" "And eight?" "And six?" And so on, till Pip was tired of answering, and quite glad when they started for Miss Havisham's.

In a quarter of an hour they reached the house, which was of old brick, and had a great many iron bars to it. Some of the windows had been walled up; of those that remained, all the lower ones were rustily barred.

There was a courtyard in front, and that was barred too; so they had to wait, after ringing the bell, until someone should come and open it.

"And fourteen?" said Mr Pumblechook, as Pip was peeping in at the gate. But Pip pretended not to hear; and he saw that at the side of the house there was a large brewery, but no brewing was going on in it.

A window was raised, and a clear voice demanded, "What name?"

"Pumblechook," answered the corn chandler.

"Quite right," answered the voice. The window was shut again, and a little girl came across the courtyard with keys in her hand.

"This," said Mr Pumblechook, "is Pip."

"This is Pip, is it?' returned the little lady, who was very pretty, and seemed very proud. "Come in, Pip."

Mr Pumblechook was coming in also, when she stopped him at the gate. "Oh!" she said, "did you wish to see Miss Havisham?"

"If Miss Havisham wished to see me," returned Mr Pumblechook, disappointed.

"Ah!" said the girl, "but you see she doesn't." She locked the gate, and Pip went with her across the courtyard. It was paved and clean, but grass was growing in every crevice.

She saw Pip looking at the brewery buildings, and she said, "You could drink without hurt all the strong beer that's brewed there now, boy?"

"I should think I could, miss," said Pip in a shy way.

"As to strong beer, there's enough of it in the cellars already to drown the Manor House."

"Is that the name of this house, miss?" said Pip.

"One of its names, boy. Its other name was Satis, which is Greek, or Latin, or Hebrew, for enough."

"Enough House," said Pip. "That's a curious name, miss.

"Yes," she replied. "It meant, when it was given, that whoever had this house could want nothing else. But don't loiter, boy."

Though she called him "boy" so often, she was about his own age; but she seemed older than Pip, being a girl, and so pretty and self-possessed. And she was as scornful of him as if she had been one-and-twenty, and a queen.

They went into the house by a side door, and the first thing Pip noticed was that the passages were all dark, and that she had left a candle burning there. She took it up, and they went through more passages, and up a staircase; and still it was all dark, and only the candle lighted them.

At last they came to the door of a room, and she said, "Go in."

"After you, miss," said Pip, shyly.

"Don't be ridiculous, boy;" she returned. "I am not going in." And she walked scornfully away.

Pip felt very uncomfortable; but he knocked at the door, and a voice bade him enter. Pip obeyed, and found himself in a pretty large room, well lighted by wax candles. No glimpse of daylight was to be seen in it. It was a dressing room; for there was a draped table with a gilded looking glass upon it; and in an arm-chair, with her elbow resting on the table, sat the strangest lady Pip had ever seen.

She was dressed in rich materials—satins, and lace, and silk—all of white. Her shoes were white. And she had a long white veil hanging from her hair, and she had bridal flowers in her hair, though her hair was white.

Jewels sparkled on her neck and on her hands, and half-packed trunks were scattered about the room. And Pip presently saw that the white dress had been white long ago, but was now faded and yellow. He saw that the bride within the bridal dress had withered like the dress; that the dress had been put upon the rounded figure of a young woman, and that the figure, upon which it now hung loose had shrunk to skin and bone.

"Who is it?" said the lady.

"Pip, ma'am," said Pip.

"Pip?"

"Mr Pumblechook's boy, ma'am. Come—to play."

"Come nearer. Let me look at you,' said the lady. "Come close."

And when Pip stood before her, he saw that her watch had stopped at twenty minutes to nine, and that a clock in the room had stopped at twenty minutes to nine.

"Look at me," said Miss Havisham. "You are not afraid of a woman who has never seen the sun since you were born?"

Pip said " No." But he was rather afraid.

"Do you know what I touch here?" she said, laying her hands on her left side.

"Your heart, ma'am," said Pip.

"Broken!" She uttered the word with a weird smile, and then took her hands away, as if they were heavy. "I am tired," she said. "I want amusement. I have done with men and women. Play. There, there!" with an impatient movement of her fingers—"play—play— play!"

Pip felt it impossible to play, and he stood looking at Miss Havisham, in what she took for a dogged manner.

"Are you sullen and obstinate?" she said.

"No, ma'am," said Pip. "I am very sorry for you, and very sorry I can't play just now. It is so new here, and so strange."

"So new to him," she muttered, "so old to me; so strange to him, so familiar to me. Call Estella. You can do that. Call Estella. At the door."

Pip felt it a dreadful liberty to bawl, "Estella!" to a scornful young lady. But she answered at last, and her light came along the dark passage like a star.

Miss Havisham beckoned her to come close, and took up a jewel, and tried its effect against the girl's hair. "Your own, one day, my dear," she said. "Let me see you play cards with this boy."

"With this boy!" said Estella. "Why, he's a common labouring boy!"

Miss Havisham whispered something in her ear. And Estella said, with the greatest disdain, "What do you play, boy?"

"Nothing but 'Beggar my neighbour,' miss," said Pip.

"Beggar him," said Miss Havisham. So they sat down to cards.

Estella dealt the cards, and Pip, glancing at the dressing table, saw beautiful jewels sparkling there, and a handkerchief, and gloves, and a Prayer-book all confusedly heaped about the looking-glass.

"He calls the knaves Jacks—this boy!" said Estella with disdain, before their first game was out. "And what coarse hands he has! And what thick boots!"

Pip had never thought of being ashamed of his hands before, but he felt ashamed now.

Estella won the game, and Pip dealt. And Pip was so abashed at her contempt for him, that he dealt wrong, and Estella called him a stupid, clumsy boy.

"You say nothing of her," remarked Miss Havisham to Pip, as she looked on. "She says many hard things of you. What do you think of her?"

"I don't like to say," stammered Pip.

"Tell me in my ear," said Miss Havisham, bending down.

"I think she is very proud," said Pip in a whisper.

"Anything else?"

"I think she is very pretty, and very insulting, and I should like to go home."

"You shall go soon," said Miss Havisham aloud. "Play the game out."

Pip played the game to an end, and Estella beggared him. And throwing the cards down on the table, when she had won them all, she looked contemptuously at Pip.

"When shall I have you here again?" said Miss Havisham. "Let me think."

"This is Wednesday—" began Pip; when Miss Havisham stopped him with an impatient movement of her fingers.

"There, there!" she said. "I know nothing of the days of the week. I know nothing of the weeks of the year. Come again after six days. You hear?"

"Yes, ma'am."

"Estella, take him down. Let him have something to eat, and let him roam and look about him while he eats. Go, Pip."

Pip followed the candle down, as he had followed the candle up, and Estella stood it in the place where he had first seen it. She opened the side entrance, and Pip, who had fancied it was night-time, was quite confounded by the strong rush of daylight.

"You are to wait here, you boy," said Estella; and she disappeared, closing the door.

Pip looked at his coarse hands and his thick boots, and he felt that they were very vulgar indeed. He determined to ask Joe why he had taught him to call those picture cards Jacks, which ought to be called knaves. And then Estella came back, with some bread and meat, and a little mug of beer.

She put the mug down on the stones in the yard, and gave him the bread and meat without looking at him, as insolently as if he were a dog in disgrace.

Pip felt so much humiliated, hurt, and angry, that the tears started to his eyes; and when she was gone—with a contemptuous toss of her head—Pip got behind one of the gates in the brewery lane, and leaned his sleeve against the wall there, and put his forehead on it, and cried. And as he cried, his feelings were so bitter that he kicked the wall, and pulled his hair; and that made him feel better.

Then he ate the bread and meat, which tasted very nice, and then he began to look about him.

It was a deserted place. The very pigeon house, in the brewery yard, had been blown crooked on its pole. And there were no horses in the stable, no pigs in the sty, no malt in the storehouse, no smells of beer in the vats.

Behind the furthest end of the brewery was a rank garden with an old wall, low enough for him to look over and see that the garden was the garden of the house, and that it was overgrown with tangled weeds.

Presently he saw Estella approaching with the keys to let him out. Opening the gate, she stood holding it, and Pip was passing out without looking at her, when she said tauntingly, "Why don't you cry?"

"Because I don't want to," said Pip.

"You do," said Estella. "You have been crying, and you're near crying now." Then she laughed, and pushed him out, and locked the gate upon him.

Pip went straight to Mr Pumblechook's; and was glad to find him not at home. So he set off on the four-mile walk to the forge. And as he went, he looked at his coarse hands very often, and also at his thick boots.

When Pip reached home, his sister was very curious to know all about Miss Havisham, and asked a number of questions. Pip had a feeling within him, that it would be mean and treacherous to show up Miss Havisham, as he had really seen her; so he said as little as he could.

This made Mrs Joe very angry, and she thumped Pip in the small of the back, and pushed him against the kitchen wall. And at that moment Mr Pumblechook turned up in his chaise cart, full of curiosity to know of all Pip had seen and heard.

"Well, boy," said Uncle Pumblechook, "how did you get on up town?"

"Pretty well, sir," said Pip.

"Pretty well is no answer, boy," said Mr Pumblechook. "What do you mean by pretty well?" And Mrs Joe shook her fist at Pip.

Pip had been so much bullied by Mrs Joe, that he thought he would not be bullied now by Mr Pumblechook, so he said obstinately, "I mean pretty well."

Mrs Joe was going to fly at Pip, when Mr Pumblechook interfered. "No! Don't lose your temper," he said. "Leave this lad to me, mum. First: Forty-three pence?"

"I don't know," said Pip.

"Is forty-three pence seven-and-sixpence three far-dens, for instance?" asked Mr Pumblechook.

"Yes!" said Pip. And Mrs Joe immediately boxed his ears.

"Boy!" said Mr Pumblechook, folding his arms tight on his chest, "what like is Miss Havisham?"

"Very tall and dark," said Pip.

"Is she, uncle?" asked Mrs Joe.

Mr Pumblechook nodded, and Pip knew at once that he had never seen Miss Havisham, for she was nothing of the kind.

"Good!" said Mr Pumblechook. "This is the way to have him, mum. Now, boy! What was she a-doing of when you went in to-day?"

"She was sitting," said Pip, "in a black velvet coach."

Mr Pumblechook and Mrs Joe stared at each other, and both repeated, "In a black velvet coach!"

"Yes," said Pip. "And Miss Estella—that's her niece, I think—handed her in cake and wine at the coach window, on a gold plate. And we all had cake and wine on gold plates."

"Was there anybody else there?" asked Mr Pumblechook.

"Four large dogs," said Pip. "And they fought for veal cutlets out of a silver basket."

Mr Pumblechook and Mrs Joe stared at each other again in utter amazement. "Where *was* this coach, in the name of gracious?" asked Mrs Joe.

"In Miss Havisham's room,' said Pip.

"Can this be possible, uncle?" said Mrs Joe.

"My opinion is, mum," said Mr Pumblechook, "it's a sedan

chair. She's flighty, you know—very flighty—quite flighty enough to pass her time in a sedan chair."

"Did you ever see her in it, uncle?" asked Mrs Joe.

"How could I," returned Mr Pumblechook, forced to admit it, "when I never seen her in my life?"

"Goodness, uncle! And yet you have spoken to her!"

"Why, don't you know," said Mr Pumblechook testily, "that when I've been there, I've been took up to the outside of her door, and the door has stood ajar, and she has spoke to me that way? What did you play at, boy?"

"We played with flags," said Pip. "Miss Estella waved a blue flag, and I waved a red one, and Miss Havisham waved one sprinkled all over with little gold stars out of the coach window. And there was no daylight in the room, for it was all lighted up with candles."

"That's true, mum," said Mr Pumblechook, with a grave nod; "for that much I've seen myself." And he and Mrs Joe were so much taken up with talking of these marvels that they talked till Joe came in from the forge for a cup of tea. And Mrs Joe immediately told Joe what Pip had said.

Now, when Pip saw Joe open his blue eyes, and roll them round the kitchen in amazement, Pip was overtaken by penitence, and was very sorry for the stories he had told. And he listened silently, while Mrs Joe and Mr Pumblechook said they had no doubt Miss Havisham would "do something" for Pip.

Joe then went back to the forge, and after Mr Pumblechook had driven off, and when Mrs Joe was washing up, Pip stole into the forge, and remained by Joe until he had done for the night.

Then he said, "Before the fire goes out, Joe, I should like to tell you something. You remember all that about Miss Havisham's, Joe?"

"Remember?" said Joe. "I believe you! Wonderful!"

"It's a terrible thing, Joe," said Pip. "It ain't true."

"What are you telling of, Pip?" cried Joe, in the greatest amazement. "You don't mean to say it's—"

"Yes, I do," said Pip. "It's lies, Joe."

"But not all of it," cried Joe. "Why, sure you don't mean to say, Pip, that there was no black velvet coach?" For Pip stood shaking his head. "But at least there was dogs, Pip. If there warn't no weal cutlets, at least there was dogs."

"No, Joe," said Pip.

"A dog," said Joe. "A puppy? Come!"

"No, Joe, there was nothing at all of the kind."

Joe looked at him in dismay. "Pip, old chap!" he said. "This won't do, old fellow! I say! Where do you expect to go to?"

"It's terrible, Joe, ain't it?"

"Terrible!' cried Joe. "Awful! What possessed you?"

"I don't know what possessed me," said Pip, hanging his head, "but I wish you hadn't taught me to call knaves at cards—Jacks; and I wish my boots weren't so thick, nor my hands so coarse."

And then Pip told Joe that he felt very miserable, and that there had been a beautiful young lady at Miss Havisham's, who was dreadfully proud, and that she had said Pip was common, and that Pip wished he was not common, and that the lies had come of it— somehow.

"There's one thing you may be sure of," said Joe, "namely, that lies is lies. Hows'ever they come, they didn't ought to come, and they come from the father of lies, and work round to the same. Don't you tell no more of 'em, Pip. That ain't the way to get out of being common, old chap. And look'ee here, Pip, at what is said to you by a true friend: if you can't get to be oncommon through going straight, you'll never get to do it through being crooked. So don't tell no more on 'em, Pip, and live well and die happy."

"You are not angry with me, Joe?" said Pip.

"No, old chap. But a sincere well-wisher would advise, that them lies should be dropped into your prayers when you go up-stairs to bed. That's all, old chap, and don't never do it no more."

When Pip got to his little room and said his prayers, he did not forget Joe's advice; and yet his mind was so much disturbed by Estella's contempt that he thought, long after he laid him down in bed, how common Estella would consider Joe—a mere blacksmith; how thick his boots, and how coarse his hands!

When he awoke next morning, the happy idea occurred to Pip that the best step he could take towards making himself uncommon was to get out of Biddy everything she knew. And that evening when he went to Mr Wopsle's great-aunt's school, he told Biddy that he had a particular reason for wishing to get on in life, and that he would be greatly obliged to her, if she would impart all her learning to him, Biddy, who was the most obliging of girls, immediately said she would, and that very night she set him some copying to do at home.

4

The Pale Young Gentleman

At the appointed time, Pip returned to Miss Havisham's, and his ring at the gate brought out Estella. She locked it after admitting Pip, and took no notice of him until she took up the candle in the dark passage, when she said—looking scornfully over her shoulder—"You are to come this way."

She took him to quite another part of the house, through a long passage, and went into a gloomy room with a low ceiling. There was some company in the room, and Estella said, "You are to go and stand there, boy, till you are wanted"—pointing to the window.

Pip crossed to the window, and stood there, feeling very uncomfortable, and looked into a most miserable corner of the neglected garden.

The people in the other part of the room stopped talking, and Pip felt they were looking at him. There were three ladies and one gentleman; and Pip learned later that they were relations of Miss Havisham's, and that they all toadied to her, and fawned upon her, because she was so rich.

Then they began talking again, and Pip heard them sneering at some gentleman who was not there, whom they called Matthew Pocket, saying that Matthew was nobody's enemy but his own.

Presently a bell rang in the distance, and Estella said to Pip, "Now, boy!"

Pip turned round, and the company looked at him with the utmost contempt; and he heard one of the ladies say, "Well, I'm sure! What next!"

And another said, "Was there ever such a fancy! The i-*de*-a!"

And Pip knew they were talking of him, and wondering what Miss Havisham wanted him in the house for.

As Estella went along the dark passage with her candle, she looked at Pip over her shoulder, and said, in her taunting manner, "Am I pretty?"

"Yes," said Pip. "I think you are very pretty,"

"Am I insulting?"

"Not so much now as you were last time," said Pip.

On their way upstairs, they met a gentleman who was groping his way down in the dark. "Whom have we here?" said he, stopping and looking at Pip.

"A boy," said Estella.

"Boy of the neighbourhood? Hey?"

"Yes, sir," said Pip.

He was a burly man, of an exceedingly dark complexion, with an exceedingly large head, and an exceedingly large hand that smelt of scented soap. He took Pip by the chin, and turned up his face to have a look at him by the light of the candle; and Pip saw that he had bushy black eyebrows, with eyes set very deep in his head, and very sharp and suspicious-looking.

"How do you come here?" he said.

"Miss Havisham sent for me, sir," explained Pip.

"Well! Behave yourself," said he, biting the side of his great forefinger, as he frowned at Pip. "Mind you behave yourself."

Then he let Pip go, and went his way downstairs; and Estella led him to Miss Havisham's room, where she and everything else were just as Pip had left them.

"Are you ready to play?" she said.

"I don't think I am, ma'am," said Pip in some confusion.

"Since you are unwilling to play," said Miss Havisham impatiently, "are you willing to work?"

Pip said readily that he was quite willing to work.

"Then go into that opposite room," said she, pointing at the door behind him, "and wait there till I come."

Pip crossed the staircase landing and entered the room opposite, which had an airless smell that was very oppressive. A fire had been just kindled in the grate, and wax candles on the high chimney-piece faintly lighted the chamber. It looked as if it had been a handsome room once; but now everything was covered with dust and mould.

In the middle of the room was a long table with a tablecloth spread on it, as if a feast had been in preparation long ago. A centrepiece of some kind was in the middle of this cloth; but it was so heavily overhung with cobwebs, that its form could not be distinguished. And, as Pip looked along the yellow cloth that had once been white, he saw speckled-legged spiders, with blotchy bodies, running in and out of the cobwebs. He heard mice, too, rattling behind the panels, while black beetles crawled about the hearth.

Presently Miss Havisham entered, looking like the witch of the place, and laid one hand on Pip's shoulder. In her other hand she had a crutch-headed stick on which she leaned.

"This," said she, pointing to the long table with her stick, "is where I will be laid when I am dead. My relations shall come and look at me here. What do you think that is?" she added— "that, where the cobwebs are?"

"I can't guess, ma'am," said Pip.

"It's a great cake," she said. "A bride-cake. Mine! Come. Walk me—walk me!"

Pip made out, from this, that the work he had to do was to walk Miss Havisham round and round the room. And she and he started off at once—the lady leaning upon the boy's shoulder.

After awhile she said, "Call Estella!" So Pip went to the landing and bawled, "Estella!" till he saw her light appear; and then Miss Havisham told him to walk her again.

Estella soon entered the room, followed by the three ladies and the gentleman whom he had seen below. Pip would have stopped, but Miss Havisham, twitching his shoulder, bade him go on.

And then the relations all began to flatter Miss Havisham. Miss Sarah Pocket—a little, dried-up, brown old woman with a large mouth like a cat's—said how well Miss Havisham looked; and another lady, whom they called Camilla, said that she thought so much of Miss Havisham when she woke up in the night, that her—Camilla's—health was suffering.

"Then don't think of me," retorted Miss Havisham.

That seemed to please Sarah Pocket; for the relations all mis-

Estella came back with some bread and meat.

Pip was at the bellows.

trusted each other, and each was anxious to inherit Miss Havisham's money, when she was dead.

Then they all abused the absent Matthew, who, as they said, never came to see how dear Miss Havisham was.

When Matthew was mentioned, Miss Havisham stopped walking. "Matthew," she said in a stern voice, "will come and see me at last when I am laid dead on that table. That will be his place—there," striking the table with her stick, "at my head ! And yours will be there, Camilla! And your husband's there! And Sarah Pocket's there! And Georgiana's there! Now you all know where to take your stations when you come to feast upon me. And now go!"

So they all trooped away, lighted by Estella. And Miss Havisham said to Pip, "This is my birthday, Pip."

Pip was going to wish her many happy returns, when she lifted her stick. "I don't suffer it to be spoken of," she said. "I don't suffer those that were here just now to speak of it. They come here on the day, but they dare not refer to it. On this day of the year, Pip, long before you were born, this heap of decay"—pointing at the pile of cobwebs in the centre of the table—"was brought here. It and I have worn away together. When I am dead, they shall lay me, in my bride's dress, on the bride's table."

She stood looking at the table till Estella returned. And then she said, "Let me see you two play cards again."

With that, they returned to the other room, and played cards as before. Having played some half-dozen games, a day was appointed for Pip's return; and he was taken down into the yard to be fed, and to be left to wander about as he liked.

A gate in the garden wall which he had scrambled up to peep over last time being open, Pip strolled into the garden and strolled all over it, when, happening to look up at one of the windows of the house, he was surprised to see a pale young gentleman with light hair, staring at him.

This pale young gentleman disappeared, and reappeared in the garden beside Pip. "Hulloa, young fellow!" he said. "Who let *you* in?"

"Miss Estella."

"Come and fight," said the pale young gentleman, who was about the same age as Pip. And Pip followed where he led, as if he were under a spell.

"Stop a minute, though," said the pale young gentleman, wheeling round. "I ought to give you a reason for fighting too. There it is!" He instantly slapped his hands against one another, daintily flung one of his legs up behind him, pulled Pip's hair, slapped his hands again, dipped his head, and butted it into Pip's stomach.

At that, Pip hit out at him, and was going to hit out again, when he said, "Aha! Would you?" And began dancing backwards and forwards.

"Laws of the game!" said he. Here he skipped from his left leg on to his right. "Regular rules!" Here he skipped from his right leg to his left. "Come to the ground, and go through the preliminaries."

Pip was secretly afraid of him, when he saw him so dexterous; but he followed him without a word into a retired nook of the garden.

"Are you satisfied with the ground?" said he.

And when Pip said, "Yes," he begged Pip's leave to absent himself for a moment, and quickly returned with a bottle of water and a sponge.

"Available for both," he said, placing these against the wall. And then he fell to pulling off, not only his jacket and waistcoat, but his shirt too, in a manner at once light-hearted and bloodthirsty.

Though he was Pip's age, he was much taller, and Pip's heart failed him when he saw him squaring at him in such a scientific manner. And Pip was quite surprised when he himself let out the first blow, and saw the pale young gentleman lying on his back, looking up at Pip with a bloody nose.

He was on his feet directly though, and, after sponging himself with a show of great dexterity, began squaring at Pip once more. Pip was surprised to see him on his back again, looking up at Pip out of a black eye.

His spirit inspired Pip with great respect. He seemed, however, to have no strength. He never once hit Pip hard, and in every round of the fight he was knocked down; but he would be up again in a moment, sponging himself, or drinking out of the water bottle; and then came at Pip with an air that made Pip believe he was going to do for him at last.

Presently he got a bad fall with his head against a wall, and then went down on his knees to his sponge, and threw it up, panting out, "That means you have won."

He seemed so brave and bright that Pip felt but a gloomy satisfaction in his victory. "Can I help you?" asked Pip.

"No, thank'ee," said he.

"Good afternoon," said Pip.

"Same to you," said he.

Pip got into the courtyard, and found Estella waiting with her keys. She neither asked Pip where he had been, nor why he had kept her waiting; but there was a bright flush upon her face as though something had happened to delight her.

"Come here," she said, stepping back into the passage, and beckoning Pip. "You may kiss me, if you like."

Pip kissed her cheek as she turned it to him. And he did not know that she had been peeping at them while they fought, and was delighted with Pip for having beaten the pale young gentleman, whom she did not like.

Pip went home, and thought a good deal of the pale young gentleman; and when the day came round for his return to Miss Havisham's, he was rather afraid, not of the pale young gentleman but of Miss Havisham, lest she should be angry with him for having made the pale young gentleman's nose bleed, and given him a black eye.

But no one alluded in any way to the fight, and no pale young gentleman was to be seen. Pip explored the garden, and looked up at the windows of the house, but no young gentleman was there.

Only in the corner of the garden where the fight had taken place, there were traces of his blood, and Pip covered them up with garden mould.

5

Apprenticed to Joe

The next time Pip went to Miss Havisham's, he saw, on the broad landing between her own room and that other room where the long table was laid out, a light chair on wheels, which was pushed from behind. And it now became Pip's duty to push Miss Havisham in this chair round her own room, and across the landing, and round the other room.

Over and over and over again they made these journeys; and it was settled that Pip should go to Miss Havisham's every second day at noon, for the purpose of wheeling her about.

As they began to be more used to one another, Miss Havisham talked more to Pip, and asked him what he had learnt, and what he was going to be. And Pip said he was to be apprenticed to Joe.

Estella was always about, but she never told Pip he might kiss her again. Sometimes she would be cold and proud, while at other times she would be quite friendly with him, and now and then she would tell him that she hated him. In this way another year passed by.

Miss Havisham would often ask him, in a whisper, "Does she grow prettier and prettier, Pip?" And when Pip said "Yes" (for indeed she did) Miss Havisham would seem to enjoy it greedily.

And sometimes, after Estella had been very disagreeable to Pip, Miss Havisham would embrace her fondly, and whisper in Estella's ear, "Break his heart, my pride and hope, and have no mercy."

But Pip did not understand that till long afterwards.

It was a strange life for Pip; and living so much, as he did, with Miss Havisham and Estella, Pip began to think that to become a blacksmith like Joe would be but a poor affair after all.

Then, too, Mrs Joe and Mr Pumblechook were always talking about Miss Havisham in front of Pip—wondering what Miss Havisham was going to do for him.

Joe was the only one who never talked about the matter; but Pip knew that Joe was not favourable to his being taken away from the forge, and Pip was fully old enough now to be apprenticed to Joe.

So that strange year at Miss Havisham's passed away, and one day Miss Havisham stopped short as she was walking with her hand on Pip's shoulder. "You are growing tall, Pip," she said. "Tell me the name again of that blacksmith of yours."

"Joe Gargery, ma'am."

"Meaning the master you were to be apprenticed to?"

"Yes, Miss Havisham."

"You had better be apprenticed at once," she said. "Would

Gargery come here with you, and bring your indentures, do you think?"

And by indentures, she meant the written agreement between a master and his apprentice.

Pip said Joe would think it an honour to come.

"Let him come soon," said Miss Havisham, "and come alone with you."

When Pip got home at night and gave Joe the message, Mrs Joe "went on the rampage," in a most alarming degree, because *she* had not been invited to Miss Havisham's too.

She asked Joe and Pip whether they supposed she was door-mats under their feet, and what company they graciously thought she was fit for? Then she threw a candlestick at Joe, and burst out sobbing.

The next day but one, Joe dressed himself in his Sunday clothes to accompany Pip to Miss Havisham's, and he pulled up his shirt collar so high behind, that it made the hair on the crown of his head stand up like a tuft of feathers.

Pip tormented himself in wondering what Miss Havisham and Estella would think of Joe, and, in his heart, he was ashamed of himself for being ashamed of Joe.

Mrs Joe said she would go to town with them, and would stop at Uncle Pumblechook's, where they could call for her when— as she added snappishly—they "had done with their fine ladies."

So the forge was shut up for the day; and Joe wrote in chalk upon the door, "HOUT," drawing a sketch of an arrow supposed to be flying in the direction he had taken.

They walked the four miles to the town, and when they came

to Mr Pumblechook's, Mrs Joe bounced in angrily and left them, while Joe and Pip went straight on to Miss Havisham's.

Estella opened the gate as usual, but took no notice of either of them, and led the way, that Pip knew so well, to Miss Havisham's room door.

"You are both to go in," she said, and made them go in first.

So Pip conducted Joe into Miss Havisham's presence, where she was seated as usual at the dressing table, in the white bride's dress that was now yellow.

"Oh!" said she to Joe. "You are the husband of the sister of this boy?"

"Which I meantersay," said Joe, turning to Pip, "as I hup and married your sister, Pip, and I were what you might call a single man."

It was very aggravating to Pip, but Joe persisted in addressing him instead of Miss Havisham.

"Well," said Miss Havisham, "and you have reared the boy with the intention of taking him for your apprentice? Does the boy like the trade?"

"Which it is well beknown to yourself, Pip," returned Joe, "that it were the wish of your own hart."

Pip made faces at him, and signed to him to address Miss Havisham, but Joe persisted in speaking to Pip.

"Have you brought his indentures with you?" asked Miss Havisham.

"Well, Pip, you know," said Joe, "you yourself see me put 'em in my 'at." With which, he took them out and gave them, not to Miss Havisham, but to Pip.

And when Pip saw that Estella stood at the back of Miss Havisham's chair, and that her eyes laughed mischievously, he was ashamed of dear, good Joe.

"You expected," said Miss Havisham, as she looked over the indentures which Pip put into her hand, "no premium with the boy?" And by premium she meant a sum of money.

"Joe," burst out Pip, "why don't you answer—"

"Pip," returned Joe—cutting him short, as if he were hurt—"which you know the answer to be full well No."

Miss Havisham glanced at Joe, as if she understood what a good fellow he really was, and that she knew he was only shy; and, taking up a little bag from the table beside her, she said:

"Pip has earned a premium here. And here it is. There are five-and-twenty guineas in this bag. Give it to your master, Pip."

It was quite impossible for Joe to address Miss Havisham. "This is very liberal on your part, Pip," said he, "and it is as such received and grateful welcome, though never looked for, far, nor near, nor nowheres. And now, old chap, may we do our duty."

"Goodbye, Pip!" said Miss Havisham. "Let them out, Estella."

"Am I to come again, Miss Havisham?" asked Pip.

"No. Gargery is your master now.—Gargery! One word!"

She called him back as Pip went out of the door, and Pip heard her say to Joe, "The boy has been a good boy here, and that is his reward. Of course, as an honest man, you will expect no more."

How Joe got out of the room, Pip never knew; but when they were outside the gate, and it was locked, and Estella was gone, Joe backed up against a wall and exclaimed:

"Astonishing! Pip, I do assure you this is as-TON-ishing!" And then they both walked on to Mr Pumblechook's.

"Well!" cried Mrs Joe, addressing both of them at once. "And what's happened to *you*! I wonder you condescend to come back to such poor society as this!"

"Miss Havisham," said Joe, with a fixed look at Pip, "made it wery particular that we should give her—were it compliments or respects, Pip?"

"Compliments," said Pip.

"Her compliments to Mrs J. Gargery, and wishing that the state of Miss Havisham's 'elth were sitch as would have—allowed, were it, Pip?"

"Of her having the pleasure," added Pip.

"Of ladies' company," said Joe. And he drew a long breath.

"Well!" cried Mrs Joe, with a gratified glance at Mr Pumblechook. "And what did she give young Rantipole here?"

"She giv' him," said Joe, "nothing. What she giv' she giv' to his friends. And by his friends she meant Mrs J. Gargery."

Mrs Joe looked at Mr Pumblechook, who nodded at her, as if he had known all about it beforehand.

"And how much have you got?" asked Mrs Joe, laughing. Positively laughing!

"What would present company say to ten pound?" demanded Joe.

"They'd say," returned Mrs Joe curtly, "pretty well. Not too much, but pretty well."

"It's more than that, then," said Joe.

And Mr Pumblechook, as if he knew all about that too, nodded again. "It's more than that, mum."

"What would present company say," proceeded Joe, "to twenty pound?"

"Handsome would be the word," returned Mrs Joe.

"Well, then," said Joe, "it's more than twenty pound."

And Mr Pumblechook said, with a patronising laugh, "It's more than that, mum."

"Then, to make an end of it," said Joe—delightedly handing the bag to Mrs Joe—"it's five-and-twenty guineas."

"It's five-and-twenty guineas, mum," echoed Mr Pumblechook, rising to shake hands with her. "And it's no more than your merits; and I wish you joy of the money! I am one of them that always go right through with what they've begun. This boy must be bound out of hand."

The Justices were sitting in the Town Hall near at hand, and they went at once to have Pip bound to Joe in the magistrates' presence.

Then they went back to Mr Pumblechook's; and Mrs Joe became so much excited, by the twenty-five guineas, that nothing would serve her but that they should have a dinner at the Blue Boar, and that Mr Pumblechook should go over in his chaise cart, and bring the Hubbles and Mr Wopsle.

After dinner they all accompanied Joe, and Mrs Joe, and Pip home; but when Pip got into his little bedroom that night, he was not happy, but very wretched, and felt that he should never like Joe's trade. Once he had liked it very much; but that was before he had known Estella.

It is a most miserable thing to feel ashamed of home and Pip *was* ashamed of home. He thought it was all coarse and common; and he would not have had Miss Havisham and Estella see it on any account.

Once it had seemed to Pip that, when he should at last roll up his shirt sleeves and go into the forge, as Joe's apprentice, he should be distinguished and happy.

Now that he really was Joe's apprentice, he only felt that he was dusty with the dust of small coal, and was haunted by the fear that, in some unlucky hour, when he was grimiest and commonest, with black face and hands, doing the coarsest part of his work, he should see Estella looking in at him at one of the wooden windows of the forge.

Of course, Pip had left Mr Wopsle's great-aunt's school, but not before Biddy had taught him all she knew herself. And now, in his great desire to improve, Pip got books and began to study them himself.

And on Sundays, when Joe and he went to sit by the old Battery on the marshes, Pip would try to teach Joe, for he wanted to make Joe less ignorant and less common.

"Joe," said Pip one Sunday after many months, "don't you think I ought to make Miss Havisham a visit?"

Joe considered for a moment. Then he said, "In regard of wisiting Miss Havisham, Pip, she might think you wanted something—expected something of her."

"Don't you think I might say that I did not, Joe?"

"You see, Pip," said Joe, "Miss Havisham done the handsome thing by you. When she done the handsome thing by you, she called me back to say to me—as that were all."

"Yes, Joe," said Pip, "I heard her."

"Which I meantersay, Pip, it might be that her meaning were—make an end of it—me to the north, and you to the south! Keep in sunders!"

"But, Joe, here I am getting on in the first year of my time, and, since the day of my being bound, I have never thanked Miss Havisham, nor asked after her, nor shown that I remember her."

"That's true, Pip."

"And, Joe, what I wanted to say was that, as we are rather slack just now, if you would give me a half-holiday tomorrow, I think I would go up town, and make a call on Miss Havisham."

"Well, old chap, if you think well of it, I think well of it," said Joe. And he consented to give the half-holiday.

Now, Joe kept a journeyman whose name was Orlick. He was a broad-shouldered, swarthy fellow of great strength, never in a hurry, and always slouching; and he lodged at a sluice keeper's out on the marshes.

Orlick was at work at the forge next day when Pip reminded Joe of his half-holiday. Orlick said nothing at the moment, for he and Joe had just got a piece of hot iron between them, and Pip was at the bellows; but by and by he said, leaning on his hammer:

"Now, master! Sure you're not a-going to favour only one of us. If Young Pip has a half-holiday, do as much for Old Orlick."

He was about twenty-five years of age, but he always spoke of himself as Old Orlick.

"Why, what'll you do with a half-holiday, if you get it?" said Joe.

"What'll *I* do with it? What'll *he* do with it? I'll do as much with it as *him*," said Orlick.

"Then, as in general you stick to your work as well as most men," said Joe, "let it be a half-holiday all round."

Pip dressed himself in his best clothes, and walking into the town, found himself ringing at Miss Havisham's gate, with a beating heart. Miss Sarah Pocket came and opened it. No Estella.

"How then? You here again?" said Miss Pocket. "What do you want?"

Pip said he had come to see how Miss Havisham was and, very reluctantly, Sarah Pocket told him to come up.

Everything was unchanged, and Miss Havisham was alone. "Well?" she said. "I hope you want nothing? You'll get nothing."

"No, indeed, Miss Havisham," said Pip. "I only wanted you to know that I am doing very well in my apprenticeship, and am always much obliged to you."

"Come now and then," she said "Come on your birthday. Ay!" she cried, suddenly turning herself round. "You are looking for Estella? Hey?"

Pip had indeed been looking for Estella, and he stammered— that he hoped she was well.

"Abroad," said Miss Havisham, "educating for a lady. Far out of reach. Prettier than ever. Admired by all who see her." And she laughed so disagreeably that Pip was not sorry to be dismissed.

As he loitered, disappointed, along the High Street, he met Mr Wopsle, who was going to have tea with Mr Pumblechook, and he persuaded Pip to go too.

It was dark when he and Mr Wopsle set off on the walk home, and soon a heavy mist began to fall. By the turnpike house they came upon a man. And both cried out, "Orlick there!"

"Ah!" said Orlick, slouching out. "I was standing by a minute, on the chance of company."

And as they all walked on together, Pip asked him if he had spent his holiday up town.

"Yes," said Orlick—"all of it. By the by, the guns is going again."

"At the Hulks?" said Pip.

"Ay! There's some of the birds flown from the cages. The guns have been going since dark. You'll hear one presently."

And they had not walked many yards further, when the well-remembered boom came towards them, deadened by the mist.

"A good night for cutting off in," remarked Orlick. And Pip thought, in silence, of that other misty evening long ago.

The way by which they approached the village took them past the Three Jolly Bargemen, which they now saw was in a state of great commotion. Mr Wopsle dropped in to ask what the matter was, and came running out in a great hurry.

"There's something wrong," said he, without stopping, "up at your place, Pip. Run all."

"What is it?" asked Pip, keeping up with him, as did Orlick also.

"The house seems to have been violently entered when Joe Gargery was out," said Mr Wopsle. "Supposed by convicts. Somebody's been attacked and hurt."

They were running too fast to speak another word, and they

63

made no stop until they reached the kitchen. It was full of people. There was a surgeon, and there was Joe, and there were a group of women—all on the floor in the middle of the kitchen.

Some of them drew back when they saw Pip; and he saw—lying without sense or movement on the bare boards, where she had been knocked down by a tremendous blow on the back of the head—Mrs Joe, destined never to be on the rampage again.

The constables and the Bow Street men from London were about the house for a week or two, and took up several wrong people. But the man that had struck down Mrs Joe could not be found. And the general belief was that a runaway convict had struck the blow.

Mrs Joe lay very ill in bed. Her sight was hurt, her hearing was hurt, and her speech no one could understand. Her memory, too, was almost gone; and when at last she came round so far as to be brought downstairs, she was so helpless that Joe had to get somebody to wait upon her and keep the house.

At this time Mr Wopsle's great-aunt dying, Biddy came and made her home at the forge, and soon became a blessing to the whole household.

Pip began to think her an extraordinary girl. She managed Mrs Joe; she managed the house; and what was stranger still, she managed to get hold of Pip's books, and to learn all that Pip was learning himself. And Pip felt he could tell things to Biddy that he would not dream of telling Joe.

"Biddy," said Pip one day (it was after his birthday, when he had been to see Miss Havisham, though he had not seen Estella), "Biddy, I want to be a gentleman."

"Oh. I wouldn't, if I were you!" she said.

"Biddy," said Pip, severely, "I have particular reasons for wanting to be a gentleman."

"You know best, Pip," said Biddy. "But don't you think you are happier as you are?"

"I am disgusted with my calling and my life," burst out Pip. "I have never taken to either since I was bound."

"I am sorry for that," said Biddy.

"The beautiful young lady at Miss Havisham's is more beautiful than anybody else ever was," said Pip; "and I admire her dreadfully; and I want to be a gentleman on her account."

"That's a pity," said Biddy; and she looked very grave. Then she added, "I am glad of one thing, and that is—that you have felt you could give me your confidence, Pip."

"I shall always tell you everything," said Pip, putting his arm round her neck, and giving her a kiss.

"Till you're a gentleman," replied Biddy.

"And that will be—never," sighed Pip.

As each birthday came round, he again visited Miss Havisham, and though these interviews lasted a very few minutes, Pip came away with one thought in his head. It was that, perhaps, Miss Havisham was going to make his fortune when his time was out with Joe.

6

Pip's Dream comes True

It was the fourth year of Pip's apprenticeship to Joe, and it was a Saturday night. And while Joe sat smoking with some friends by the fire of the Three Jolly Bargemen, a strange gentleman came in.

He had an air of authority, and as he walked up towards the fire, he stood with his left hand in his pocket biting the forefinger of his right.

"From information I have received," said he, looking round the room, "I have reason to believe there is a blacksmith among you, by name Joseph Gargery. Which is the man?"

"Here is the man," said Joe.

"You have an apprentice, commonly known as Pip? Is he here?"

"I am here," answered Pip, for he had come in to fetch Joe.

The stranger did not recognize Pip, but Pip recognized him as the gentleman he had met on the stairs, when Estella was taking him up to Miss Havisham's room. And as he put his hand on Pip's shoulder, Pip noticed his large hand, his dark complexion, his deep-set eyes, his bushy black eyebrows, and even the smell of scented soap on his great hand.

"I wish to have a private talk with you two," said he, after he had looked well at Pip. "Perhaps we had better go to your own house."

Amidst a wondering silence, Joe and Pip walked with him out of the inn, and, in a wondering silence, walked home.

As they neared the forge, Joe went on ahead to open the front door, and the three entered the little parlour, which was feebly lighted by a candle.

The strange gentleman sat down at the table, drew the candle to him, and looked over some entries in his pocketbook.

Then he said, "My name is Jaggers, and I am a lawyer in London. I have unusual business to transact with you."

Finding that he could not see them very well from where he sat, Mr Jaggers got up, and threw one leg over the back of a chair, and leaned upon it, thus having one foot on the seat of the chair and one foot on the ground.

"Now, Joseph Gargery, I am the bearer of an offer to relieve you of this young fellow, your apprentice. You would not object to cancel his indentures at his request and for his good? You would not want anything for so doing?"

"Lord forbid that I should want anything for not standing in Pip's way," said Joe, staring.

"Lord forbidding is pious," returned Mr Jaggers, "but not to the purpose. The question is, Do you want anything?"

"The answer is," said Joe sternly, "No."

"Very well," said Mr Jaggers. "Recollect what you have said, and don't try to go from it presently."

"Who's a-going to try?" retorted Joe.

"I don't say anybody is. Bear in mind that Brag is a good dog, but Holdfast is a better. And what I have to tell you is—that this young fellow has Great Expectations."

Joe and Pip gasped, and looked at one another.

"I am instructed to tell him," said Mr Jaggers throwing his finger at him sideways, "that he will come into a handsome property. Further, that it is the wish of the present possessor of this property, that he be immediately removed from the forge, and be brought up as a gentleman—in a word, as a young fellow of Great Expectations."

Pip's dream was out! Miss Havisham was going to make his fortune indeed!

"Now, Mr Pip," proceeded the lawyer, "you are to understand, first, that it is the request of the person from whom I take my instructions that you always bear the name of Pip. Secondly, you are to understand that the name of your liberal benefactor remain a profound secret, until the person chooses to reveal it. Thirdly, you are to understand that you are positively forbidden to try and find out who your benefactor is. If you have a suspicion in your own breast, keep that suspicion in your own breast. The secret is solely help by your benefactor and me. If you have any objection to these conditions, this is the time to mention it Speak out."

Pip stammered, with difficulty, that he had no objection.

"I should think not!" said Mr Jaggers. "Now, Mr Pip, there is lodged in my hands a sum of money amply sufficient for your suitable education and means of living. You will please consider me your guardian."

Pip began to thank him.

"Oh!" interrupted Mr Jaggers, "I tell you at once, I am paid for my services, or I shouldn't give them. It is considered that you should be better educated, to suit your altered position."

"I have always longed for it," began the excited Pip.

"Are you ready to be placed at once under some tutor?" said Mr Jaggers.

"Yes," stammered Pip.

"Have you ever heard of any tutor whom you would prefer to another?"

As Pip had never heard of any tutor but Biddy and Mr Wopsle's great-aunt, he replied, "No."

"There is a certain tutor of whom I have some knowledge, who might suit the purpose," said Mr Jaggers. "The gentleman I speak of is one Mr Matthew Pocket."

Ah! Pip caught up the name directly. Miss Havisham's relation. The Matthew whose place was to be at Miss Havisham's head when she lay dead, in her bride's dress, on the bride's table. And thanking Mr Jaggers, he said he would gladly try that gentleman.

"Good!" returned Mr Jaggers. "You had better try him at his own house. The way shall be prepared for you, and you can see his son first, who is in London. When will you come to London?"

Pip said—glancing at Joe, who stood looking on motionless—that he supposed he could come directly.

"First," said Mr Jaggers, "you must have some new clothes to come in. Say this day week. You'll want some money. Shall I leave you twenty guineas?"

He took his leg off the chair, produced a long purse, counted the money out on the table, and pushed it over to Pip. And then he looked at Joe.

"Well, Joseph Gargery! You look dumfounded!"

"I *am*," said Joe.

"It was understood that you wanted nothing for yourself, remember?"

"It were understood," said Joe. "And it are understood."

"But what," said Mr Jaggers, swinging his purse, "if it was in my instructions to make you a present as compensation for the loss of his services?"

Joe laid his hand upon Pip's shoulder with the touch of a woman. "Pip is that hearty welcome," said he, "to go free with his services to honour and fortin', as no words can ever tell him. If you think money can make compensation to me for the loss of the little child—what came to the forge—" Joe stopped with his great arm before his eyes, his broad chest heaving, and his voice dying away.

"Now, Joseph Gargery, I warn you this is your last chance." said Mr Jaggers. "If you mean to take a present, speak out. If, on the contrary, you mean to say—"

"Which I meantersay," interrupted Joe, doubling up his fists, "that if you come into my place bull-baiting and badgering me, come out! Which I meantersay as sech if you're a man, come on!"

Mr Jaggers rose and backed near the door, and Pip put his hand on Joe's arm.

"Well, Mr Pip," said Mr Jaggers from the doorway, "I think the sooner you leave here—as you are to be a gentleman—the better. Let it stand for this day week. And then you must come straight to me. I am paid for all I undertake. Understand that."

And thinking, perhaps, that Joe still looked dangerous, he went off.

Pip, with his head full of Miss Havisham, ran after him. "Hulloa!" said Mr Jaggers, facing round. "What's the matter?"

"I wish to be quite right, Mr Jaggers," said Pip, "and to keep to your directions. Would there be any objection to my taking leave of anyone up town before I go away?"

"No," said Mr Jaggers. "No objection."

Pip thanked him, and ran home again, and found Joe seated by the kitchen fire, gazing intently at the burning coal.

Mrs Joe—whose temper had greatly improved—was in her cushioned chair in her corner, and Biddy sat at her needlework close by. Joe said nothing, and Pip sat down; but Pip could not say a word. Like Joe, he, too, stared at the fire. He felt he could not look at Joe.

At length Pip managed to say, "Joe, have you told Biddy?"

"No, Pip," returned Joe, still gazing at the fire, "which I left to yourself, Pip."

"I would rather you told, Joe," said Pip.

"Pip's a gentleman of fortin', then," said Joe. "And God bless him in it."

Biddy dropped her work and looked at Pip. And, after a pause, she and Joe began to congratulate him heartily, but there was a touch of sadness in their voices.

Pip, then, began to talk very fast, and tried to impress Biddy how important it was that nothing should be said to their friends about the person who had made his fortune.

"It will all come out in good time," said Pip rather grandly.

Biddy looked at the fire, and said she would be very particular. And Joe added, "I'll be ekervally partickler, Pip."

And then Biddy tried to make Mrs Joe understand what had happened. But though poor Mrs Joe nodded her head, and repeated, "Pip," and "property," a great many times, she did not know what it really meant.

Joe and Biddy then talked about Pip's going away, and about what they should do without him. And Pip knew in his heart that he was glad to be going away, and ashamed in his heart that he was so glad to go.

"I have been thinking, Joe," said Pip, as they sat at their supper of bread and cheese and beer, "that when I go up town on Monday and order my new clothes, I shall tell the tailor that I'll have them sent to Mr Pumblechook's, and put them on there. It would be very disagreeable to be stared at by all the people here."

"Have you thought about when you'll show yourself to Mr Gargery, and your sister, and me?" said Biddy quickly. "You will show yourself to us, won't you?"

"If you had waited another moment, Biddy," replied Pip, resentfully, "you would have heard me say that I shall bring my clothes here in a bundle one evening— most likely on the evening before I go away."

Biddy said no more, and Pip, bidding them goodnight, went upstairs; and looking round his little room, he thought what a mean little room it was, and wondered about the grand rooms he would soon be going to.

Presently he opened his window wide and looked out, and then he saw Joe come slowly forth, and take a turn or two in the air. Then Biddy brought out a pipe and lighted it for him, and Joe, who never smoked so late at night, smoked this evening, as though he wanted comforting. And Pip, drawing away from the window, crept to bed.

Next morning, after breakfast, Joe brought out Pip's indentures, and put them into the fire, and Pip felt that he was free.

"You may be sure, dear Joe," said he, "that I shall never forget you."

"No, no, Pip!" returned Joe. "*I*'m sure of that.'

And to Biddy, Pip said, when they were alone together in the garden, "I have a favour to ask of you, Biddy. It is to help Joe on a little when I am gone."

"How help him on?" asked Biddy.

"Joe is a dear, good fellow," replied Pip. "But he is rather backward in his learning and his manners."

"Oh! His manners! Won't his manners do, then?" said Biddy.

"You won't hear me out," answered Pip, snappishly. And he went on to say how, when he fully came into his property, he would want to remove Joe to a higher position —a position that his present manners would not suit.

"Have you never considered that he may be proud?" said Biddy, looking very steadily at Pip.

"Proud!" repeated Pip.

'He may be too proud," went on Biddy, "to let anyone take him out of a place that he is competent to fill, and fills well, and with respect."

That made Pip angry. He said Biddy was envious on account of his rise of fortune. And flinging himself out of the garden gate, he went for a stroll, and was very moody all day.

The next morning, Pip, putting on his best clothes, went into the town and presented himself before Mr Trabb the tailor.

Mr Trabb, who was having his breakfast in the parlour behind the shop, did not think it worth his while to come out to Pip, but called Pip in to him.

"Well," said he in a hail-fellow-well-met kind of way, "what can I do for you?"

"Mr Trabb," said Pip, "I don't want to boast, but I've come into a handsome property."

"Bless my soul!" ejaculated Mr Trabb, getting up from the table.

"I am going up to my guardian in London," said Pip, drawing some guineas out of his pocket and looking at them, "and I want a fashionable suit of clothes to go in."

"My dear sir," said Mr Trabb, bowing respectfully, "will you do me the favour of stepping into the shop?"

Mr Trabb's boy was sweeping the shop, and as Pip came in with the tailor, the boy not only swept the dust over Pip, but he knocked the broom against everything, as if to say he was equal to any blacksmith alive or dead.

"Hold that noise," said Mr Trabb sternly, "or I'll knock your head off!—Do me the favour to be seated, sir."

Pip sat down, and Mr Trabb took down a roll of cloth, ordering the boy, at the same time, to fetch other rolls. And when Pip had chosen the materials for a suit, he re-entered the parlour to be measured.

Then Mr Trabb agreed to send the suit to Mr Pumblechook's on the Thursday morning, and, bowing Pip out of the shop, he said, "Good morning, sir; much obliged."

Pip then went to the hatter's, and the bootmaker's, and the hosier's, and then directed his steps towards Mr Pumblechook's.

Mr Pumblechook—who had happened to call at the forge that very morning, and had heard the news—held out both his hands to Pip. "I give you joy of your good fortun', my dear young friend," he said. "Well deserved! Well deserved! To think," he added, "that I should have been the humble instrument of leading up to this proud reward!"

For he, too, guessed that Miss Havisham was the person who had made Pip's fortune, and *he* had been the first to mention Pip to her.

Pip hastily begged him to remember that nothing was to be ever said, or hinted, about the maker of his fortune, and Mr Pumblechook nodded knowingly.

Then he shook hands with Pip a great many times, and made Pip sit down to a little luncheon of chicken and tongue which he had ordered in from the Blue Boar. And after helping Pip to the liver wing of the chicken and the best slice of the tongue, he asked, quite tenderly, if Pip remembered their boyish games at sums; and added that he had always said of Pip, "That boy is no common boy, and, mark me, his fortun' will be no common fortun'!"

And Pip felt so big with his own importance, that he thought, perhaps, he had been mistaken in Mr Pumblechook all this time, and that he was really a sensible, good-hearted, prime fellow.

Then he shook hands again with Pip; and it was arranged that Pip should go there on Friday, first to put on his new clothes, and then to call and say goodbye to Miss Havisham.

When Friday came, Pip was conducted to Mr Pumblechook's own room to dress in, and, feeling suddenly abashed in his grand suit, he went by all the back ways to Miss Havisham's, and rang the bell.

Sarah Pocket came to the gate, and positively reeled when she saw him so much changed. "*You?*" she said. "Good gracious! What do you want?"

"I am going to London, Miss Pocket," said Pip, "and I want to say goodbye to Miss Havisham."

She took him upstairs to the room with the long spread table, where he found Miss Havisham leaning on her stick.

"Don't go, Sarah," she said. "Well, Pip?"

"I thought you would kindly not mind my taking leave of you," said Pip, looking at her with the thanks he dared not speak.

"This is a gay figure, Pip," said she, making her stick play round Pip, as if she, the fairy godmother who had changed him, were bestowing the finishing gift.

"I have come into such good fortune," murmured Pip. "And I am so grateful for it, Miss Havisham."

"Ay, ay!" said she, looking at the envious Miss Pocket, with delight. "I have seen Mr Jaggers. I have heard about it, Pip. And you are adopted by a rich person?"

"Yes, Miss Havisham."

"Well," she went on, "you have a promising career before you. Be good, and abide by Mr Jaggers's instructions. Goodbye, Pip! You will always keep the name of Pip, you know."

She stretched out her hand, and Pip, in his gratitude, went down on one knee, and put it to his lips.

She looked at Sarah Pocket with triumph in her eyes, and so Pip left his fairy godmother, standing in the midst of the dimly lighted room, beside the rotten bride-cake that was hidden in the cobwebs.

Pip then went back to Mr Pumblechook's, took off his new clothes, made them into a bundle, and returned home in his old dress.

It was his last evening at the forge, and dressing himself again in his grand suit to please Joe and Biddy, he sat in splendour until bedtime. But notwithstanding that they had roast fowl for supper, and some flip to finish with, they all felt very low, and parted for the night with heavy hearts.

They had a hurried breakfast next morning, for the coach started early, and the breakfast seemed to Pip to have no taste. And then he kissed Mrs Joe, who was laughing and nodding in her chair, and kissed Biddy, and threw his arms around Joe's neck.

And taking up his little portmanteau, he walked out; and hearing a scuffle behind him, he looked back and saw Joe throwing an old shoe after him, and Biddy throwing another.

He stopped to wave his hat, and good Joe waved his strong right arm above his head. "Hurroar!" he cried in a husky voice. And Biddy put her apron to her face.

Pip walked on and tried to whistle, but presently he broke down and cried instead. Crying, however, made him feel better; and after he had dashed his tears away, and looked back again, Joe and Biddy were out of sight.

7

Mr Pocket, Junior

The journey to London took about five hours, and it was a little past midday when the four-horse stagecoach arrived at Cheapside.

Mr Jaggers had sent Pip his address. It was Little Britain; and he had written after it on his card, "Just out of Smithfield, and close by the coach office."

Pip engaged a hackney coach and drove there, and soon it stopped in a gloomy street at certain offices with an open door, on which was painted "MR JAGGERS."

Pip went into the front office, with his little portmanteau in his hand, and asked for Mr Jaggers.

"He is in Court at present," answered the clerk. "Am I addressing Mr Pip?"

"Yes," said Pip.

"Mr Jaggers left word, would you wait in his room. He has a case on," said the clerk. And opening a door, he ushered Pip into an inner chamber at the back.

Pip sat there till he grew tired, and telling the clerk he would take a turn in the air, he went into the street and found his way into Bartholomew Close. And now he became aware that other people were waiting about for Mr Jaggers as well as he. And from scraps of conversation that he heard, he guessed that these were clients of Mr Jaggers—people who wanted to apply to him, as a lawyer, for his advice. And they all spoke of him as if he were a very great lawyer indeed.

At length Pip saw Mr Jaggers coming across the road towards him, and the waiting clients, seeing him at the same time, there was quite a rush at him.

Mr Jaggers put a hand on Pip's shoulder, and walking him on at his side, without saying anything to him, addressed himself to his followers.

Some he would have nothing to do with at all, and these lamented loudly that they could not secure the services of the great Mr Jaggers. He told others that their cases were in good hands, and they were not to bother him any more.

In this way they reached the office, and Pip's guardian, taking him into his own room, informed him what arrangements he had made for him.

Pip was to go to "Barnard's Inn" to young Mr Pocket's rooms, where he was to remain with young Mr Pocket until Monday. On Monday he was to go with him to his father's house on a visit, that he might try how he liked it. He was also told what his allowance would be, and Mr Jaggers handed him a quarter's money then and there.

"Shall I send for a coach?" asked Pip.

But his guardian answered, that it was not worth while, and that Wemmick should walk there with him. Wemmick was the clerk in the other room, and Pip accompanied him into the street.

Pip runs after Mr Jaggers.

Wemmick was a short man with a square wooden face, glittering eyes—small, keen, and black—and thin, wide lips; and he was between forty and fifty years old.

"So you were never in London before?" said Mr Wemmick.

"No," said Pip. And he asked him if he knew where Mr Matthew Pocket lived.

"Yes," was the reply. "At Hammersmith, west of London. Five miles from here."

Pip had supposed that Barnard's Inn was an hotel kept by Mr Barnard, but when they arrived at the place, he found it to be a dingy collection of shabby buildings in a melancholy little square.

Mr Wemmick led Pip into a corner, and conducted him up a flight of stairs to a set of chambers on the top floor. "Mr Pocket, Jun." was painted on the door, and there was a label on the letterbox, "Return shortly."

"He hardly thought you would come so soon," Mr Wemmick explained. "You don't want me any more?"

"No, thank you," said Pip.

"As I keep the cash," Mr Wemmick said, "we shall most likely meet pretty often. Good day."

"Good day," returned Pip. And after the clerk had gone, Pip hung about the landing waiting for Mr Pocket, Junior.

Presently he heard footsteps on the stairs, and a young gentleman about his own age came up. He had a paper bag under each arm, and a basket of strawberries in one hand, and was out of breath. "Mr Pip?" said he.

"Mr Pocket?" said Pip.

"Dear me!" he exclaimed. "I am extremely sorry. The fact is I thought, coming from the country, you might like a little fruit after dinner, and I went to Covent Garden Market to get it good."

Pip felt as if his eyes would start out of his head. He began to think this was a dream.

"Pray come in," said Mr Pocket, Junior. "Allow me to lead the way. I am rather bare here, but I hope you'll be able to make out pretty well till Monday. My father thought you would get on more agreeably through tomorrow with me than with him, and might like to take a walk about London. As to our lodging, it's not by any means splendid, because I have my own bread to earn. This is our sitting room. This is my little bedroom: rather musty, but Barnard's is musty. This is your bedroom. The furniture is hired for the occasion, but I trust it will answer the purpose. We shall be alone together, but we shan't fight, I dare say."

As he turned to smile at Pip, *his* eyes looked as if they were starting out of his head. He fell back. "Good gracious! You're the prowling boy!" he said.

"And you," said Pip, "are *the pale young gentleman!*"

They stood staring at each other, until they both burst out laughing.

"The idea of its being you!" said Herbert Pocket.

"The idea of its being *you!!*" retorted Pip.

"You hadn't come into your good fortune at that time," said Herbert.

"No," said Pip.

"*I* was rather on the lookout for good fortune then," said Herbert. "Miss Havisham had sent for me, to see if she could take a fancy to me. But she didn't."

Pip answered politely that he was surprised to hear that.

Herbert laughed. "Yes, she had sent for me on a trial visit, and if I had come out of it successfully, I suppose *I* should have had the fortune. Perhaps I should have been engaged to marry Estella."

Pip did not like that last sentence at all. He looked grave. "How did you bear your disappointment?" he asked.

"Pooh!" said Herbert. "I didn't care much for it. She's a Tartar. That girl's hard and haughty to the last degree, and has been brought up by Miss Havisham to wreak revenge on all the male sex."

"What relation is she to Miss Havisham?" asked Pip.

"None," said Herbert. "Only adopted."

"Why should she wreak revenge on all the male sex?" asked Pip.

"Good gracious, Mr Pip, don't you know?" said Herbert. "It's quite a story, and shall be saved till dinner time. Mr Jaggers is your guardian, isn't he?"

"Yes," said Pip.

And then Herbert told him that Mr Jaggers was Miss Havisham's lawyer, and that she confided entirely in him. Also that his (Herbert's) father was Miss Havisham's cousin; and that while all Miss Havisham's other relations fawned on her in the hope of getting her money when she was dead, Mr Matthew Pocket persisted in never going near her.

Herbert had such a frank and easy way with him that Pip presently told him all his little story, and laid stress on his being forbidden to inquire who his benefactor was. He also mentioned that he had been brought up a blacksmith in a country place, and knew very little of the ways of politeness, and would take it as a great kindness if Mr Pocket would give him a hint whenever he saw him doing anything wrong.

"With pleasure," was the reply. And he begged Pip to call him by his Christian name—Herbert.

Pip said he would. "My Christian name is Philip," he added.

"I don't take to Philip," returned Herbert, smiling "I'll tell you what I should like. We are so harmonious; and you have been a blacksmith—would you mind?"

"I shouldn't mind anything that you propose," answered Pip.

"There's a charming piece of music by Handel, called 'The Harmonious Blacksmith'. May I call you Handel?"

"I should like it very much," said Pip.

"Then, my dear Handel," said Herbert, turning round, as the door was opened by a waiter, "here is the dinner."

It was a very nice little dinner, and had been sent in from the coffee house. And what made the feast more delightful to Pip was the gipsy fashion in which it was served; for, there being no sideboard in the room, the waiter had to put the covers on the floor (where he fell over them), the melted butter in the arm-chair, the bread on the bookshelves, and the cheese in the coal scuttle.

As the dinner proceeded, Pip reminded Herbert of his promise to tell him about Miss Havisham.

"I'll redeem it at once," said Herbert. "But let me say first, Handel, that in London it is not the custom to put the knife into the mouth. It is scarcely worth mentioning, but it's as well to do as other people do. Also, the spoon is not used overhand, but under. You get at your mouth better."

He said it in such a lively way, that they both laughed, and Pip scarcely blushed.

"And now," said Herbert, "about Miss Havisham. Her mother died when she was a baby; and her father—a very rich brewer—denied her nothing. She had a stepbrother, for her father married again; and the second wife also died. As the son grew a young man, he turned out riotous and extravagant—altogether bad—and at last his father disinherited him. But he softened when he was dying, and left him well off, though not nearly so well off as Miss Havisham.

"Miss Havisham was now an heiress, and was looked upon as a great match. But her stepbrother—rich once more—wasted his money most fearfully again. They were bad friends, he having a great grudge against her, thinking that she had fanned his father's anger against him.

"And, now, there appeared on the scene a certain man—a friend of her stepbrother's—who courted Miss Havisham; a man who professed to be devoted to her. And I have heard my father say that she loved him passionately, and perfectly idolized him. And he practised so much on her affection, that he got great sums of money from her. The marriage day was fixed, the wedding dresses were bought, the wedding guests were invited. The day came, but not the bridegroom. He wrote her a letter—"

"Which she received," Pip struck in, "when she was dressing for her marriage? At twenty minutes to nine?"

"At the hour and minute," answered Herbert, nodding, "at which she afterwards stopped all the clocks. What was in the letter, I can't tell you, because I don't know—except that he most heartlessly broke the marriage off. She had a bad illness, and when she recovered, she laid the whole place waste, as you have seen it, and she has never since looked upon the light of day.

"It has been supposed that the man she loved and her stepbrother planned together to rob her; that it was a conspiracy between them; and that they shared the profits."

"What became of the two men ?" asked Pip.

"They fell into deeper degradation and ruin."

"You said just now, that Estella was not related to Miss Havisham, but adopted. When adopted?" asked Pip.

Herbert shrugged his shoulders. "There has been an Estella ever since I can remember," he said. "And now you know all that I know. And as to your fortune, Handel, or how you came by it—well, you may be sure *I* shall never inquire into that matter, nor my father either."

He said this with great delicacy, but with so much meaning, too, that Pip felt he as perfectly understood Miss Havisham to be the benefactress, as Pip understood the fact himself.

And now they both became very gay and sociable, and Pip asked him what he was. Herbert explained that he was at present in a counting house, and was looking about him, and that he hoped, in time, to become an insurer of ships, and trade to the East Indies.

"An interesting trade," added Herbert, "and the profits are *tremendous.*"

"Is the counting house profitable?" asked Pip.

"Why, n-no," said Herbert. "But the thing is, that you look about you. *That's* the grand thing. Then the time comes when you see your opening. And you go in, and you swoop upon it, and you make your capital, and—there you are!"

They got on famously together. In the evening they went for a walk in the streets, and went half-price to the theatre. And next day they went to church at Westminster Abbey, and in the afternoon they walked in the parks. The forge, to Pip, seemed very far off. It seemed months since he had left Joe and Biddy.

On Monday morning Herbert went to the counting house, and in the afternoon Pip and he took coach for Hammersmith, and then walked to Mr Pocket's house.

Lifting the latch of a gate, they passed direct into a little garden overlooking the river, where Mr Pocket's younger children were playing about. Mrs Pocket was sitting on a garden chair under a tree, reading, and to her Herbert introduced young Mr Pip.

Then Mr Pocket came out of the house to make Pip's acquaintance, saying he was glad to see Pip, and he hoped Pip was not sorry to see him. "For I really am not," he added, with Herbert's smile, "an alarming personage."

He was a young-looking man, but his hair was very grey, and his manner was natural and unaffected. After talking cordially with Pip, he took him into the house, and showed him his room, which was a very pleasant one.

He then knocked at the doors of two other rooms, and introduced Pip to two other of his pupils, by name Drummle and Startop. Drummle, an old-looking, heavy young man, was whistling. Startop, younger in years, was reading and holding his head, as if he thought it might explode with too strong a charge of knowledge.

That evening there was rowing on the river. As Drummle and Startop had each a boat, Pip resolved to set up a boat too, and to cut them both out, and he engaged a Thames boatman to give him lessons in rowing.

After two or three days, when Pip had settled down, Mr Pocket had a long talk with him. He told Pip, that Mr Jaggers had informed him that Pip was not to study for any profession, but that he should be well enough educated to "hold his own" with other young men in prosperous circumstances.

And he was so zealous and honourable in fulfilling his duties, as a tutor to Pip, that he made Pip zealous and honourable in fulfilling his duties as a pupil. And Pip began to work in earnest.

But Pip had taken a great liking for Herbert, and Herbert had such easy, charming manners that Pip felt his own manners would be greatly improved if he had more of Herbert's society, and he asked Mr Pocket if it was possible for him to keep his bedroom in Barnard's Inn, and come down to Hammersmith after breakfast.

Mr Pocket did not object to this arrangement at all, but suggested that Pip should first consult his guardian. So Pip went off to Little Britain, and spoke to Mr Jaggers.

"If I could buy the furniture now hired for me," said Pip, "I should be quite at home there."

"Go it!" said Mr Jaggers, with a short laugh. "Well, how much money do you want?"

"I hardly know," said Pip.

"Come!" retorted Mr Jaggers. "Fifty pounds?"

"Oh! Not nearly as much," said Pip.

"Five pounds?" said Mr Jaggers.

Pip's face fell "Oh! More than that," he said.

"More than that, eh?" retorted Mr Jaggers. "How much more? Twice five; will that do? Three times five; will that do? Four times five; will that do?"

"That will do handsomely," said Pip.

"Four times five will do handsomely, will it?" said Mr Jaggers, knitting his brows. "Wemmick," he added, opening his office door, "take Mr Pip's written order, and pay him twenty pounds." And Mr Jaggers left the office.

"I hardly know what to make of Mr Jaggers's manners, Mr Wemmick," said Pip doubtfully.

"Tell him that, and he'll take it as a compliment," answered Wemmick. "He don't mean that you *should* know what to make of it."

"I suppose he's very skilful," said Pip.

"Deep," answered Wemmick, "as Australia." Then he spoke a good deal of Mr Jaggers's cleverness, and became so friendly with Pip that he invited him to come and see him some day at his own house, at Walworth—where he had a bit of a garden and a summerhouse.

Pip said he should be delighted to go. And Mr Wemmick asked if he had dined with Mr Jaggers yet.

"Not yet," said Pip.

"Well," said Wemmick, "when you go to dine with Mr Jaggers—look at his housekeeper."

"Shall I see something very uncommon?" asked Pip.

"You'll see," answered Wemmick, "a wild beast tamed."

8

Joe's Visit

Bentley Drummle was a sulky fellow—idle, niggardly, and suspicious. He came of rich people, and was proud, too. Pip did not like him at all. But he took very kindly to Startop.

Startop and he would pull homewards on their boating evenings abreast of one another, talking in a friendly fashion; while Drummle came up in their wake alone.

It was Herbert, though, who was Pip's intimate companion and friend, and Pip gave him a half-share in his boat. Herbert often rowed down in it to Hammersmith; and as Pip had a half-share in Herbert's chambers, Pip of course was often up in London.

"So you haven't dined with Mr Jaggers yet?" said Wemmick, one day when Pip was spending the evening at his little place at Walworth.

"Not yet," said Pip.

"I expect you'll have an invitation tomorrow," said Wemmick. "He's going to ask your pals, too. Three of them. Ain't there?"

Pip did not count Drummle as a friend. But he answered, "Yes."

"Well, he's going to ask the whole gang," said Wemmick.

And the very next day, when Pip went to the office, Mr Jaggers called him into his room, where he was washing his hands with scented soap, and gave Pip the invitation for himself and friends.

"No ceremony," added Mr Jaggers, "and no dinner dress, and say tomorrow."

So at half-past six next evening, Pip and his friends presented themselves at Mr Jaggers's house—a rather stately place in Gerard Street, Soho.

Dinner was laid in a dark brown room on the first floor, and at the side of Mr Jaggers's chair was a large dumbwaiter, or side table, with a variety of bottles and decanters on it, and four dishes of fruit for dessert.

"Pip," said he, putting his large hand on Pip's shoulder, and moving him into the window, "I don't know one of your friends from the other. Who's the blotchy, sprawly, sulky fellow?"

"That's Bentley Drummle," said Pip. "The one with the delicate face is Startop."

"Bentley Drummle is his name, is it?" said Mr Jaggers. And he immediately crossed the room to talk to him. And while Pip was looking at them, surprised that his guardian should take an interest in Drummle, there came between him and them the housekeeper, with the first dish for the table.

She was a woman of about forty years of age, rather tall, with a light, graceful figure. She was extremely pale, with large faded eyes, and a quantity of streaming hair. Her lips were parted, as if she were panting, and her face bore a curious expression of suddenness and flutter.

She set the dish on the table, touched Mr Jaggers quietly on the arm, as if to call his attention to the fact that dinner was ready, and vanished.

There was fish, and a joint of choice mutton afterwards, and then an equally choice bird; while sauces and wines were given out by the host from his dumbwaiter.

No other attendant than the housekeeper appeared. She set on every dish. And Pip observed that whenever she was in the room she kept her eyes attentively on his guardian, watching him, in a kind of fear.

The dinner went off gaily, and when they got to the cheese, the conversation turned upon the rowing feats of the young men.

"As to skill," said Drummle, in his heavy, boasting fashion, and turning to Mr Jaggers, "I am more than their master; and as to strength, I could scatter them like chaff."

He became quite ferocious about it, and fell to baring and spanning his arm, to show how muscular it was. And at that they all began to bare and span their arms.

Now, the housekeeper was at that time clearing the table, and Mr Jaggers was leaning back in his chair, biting the side of his forefinger, and watching Drummle. Suddenly, he clapped his large hand on the housekeeper's like a trap, as she stretched it across the table.

"If you talk of strength," said Mr Jaggers, "I'll show you a wrist. Molly, let them see your wrist."

Her entrapped hand was on the table, but she had already put her other hand behind her waist. "Master!" she said in a low voice, with her eyes entreatingly fixed on him. "Don't."

"Molly," said Mr Jaggers, not looking at her, but at the other side of the room, "let them see *both* your wrists. Come!"

He took his hand from hers, and turned that wrist up on the table. She brought her other hand from behind her, and held the two out side by side. The last wrist was much disfigured— deeply scarred and scarred across and across.

"There's power here," said Mr Jaggers. "Very few men have the power of wrist that this woman has. That'll do, Molly, you can go now."

She withdrew her hands, and went out of the room; and Mr Jaggers, putting the decanters on from his dumbwaiter, passed round the wine.

It might have been a month after this that Pip received a letter from Biddy, saying that Joe was coming to London, and would be glad to see Pip.

Pip did not feel glad himself; indeed, he was greatly disturbed. He wondered what Herbert would think of Joe.

Pip had, lately, not only refurnished the chambers at Barnard's Inn most splendidly, but had also started a boy in top-boots, and had dressed him in a blue coat, canary waistcoat, white cravat, and creamy breeches. And Pip had become so very grand himself that he thought Joe would not only feel out of place there, but would be out of place as well.

Joe was to arrive in time for breakfast and spend the day; and as the hour approached, Pip would have liked to run away; but

Pepper—the boy in top-boots—was already in the hall, and presently he heard Joe upon the stairs.

"Mr Gargery!" announced Pepper presently. And, with his good, honest face all glowing and shining, Joe entered the room.

"Pip, how AIR you, Pip?" And catching Pip's two hands, he shook them as if he would never let them go. "Which you have that growed," said Joe, "and that swelled, and that gentlefolked; as to be sure you are a honour to your king and country."

"And you, Joe," returned Pip, trying to speak affectionately, but looking very uneasy and stiff, "look wonderfully well."

"Thank God," replied Joe, "I'm ekerval to most. And your sister, she's no worse than she were. And Biddy, she's ever right and ready." And, as he spoke, Herbert entered.

Pip presented Joe. And Joe said, "Your servant, sir." And then they sat down to breakfast.

"Do you take tea or coffee, Mr Gargery?" asked Herbert, in his pleasant voice.

"Thank'ee, sir," said Joe, stiff from head to foot, "I'll take whichever is most agreeable to you."

"What do you say to coffee?" said Herbert.

"Thank'ee, sir," returned Joe, "since you are so kind as to make chice of coffee, I will not run contrairy to your opinions." And, in his nervousness—for he felt that Pip was ashamed of him—poor Joe sat so far from the table, and dropped so much more than he ate, and pretended he hadn't dropped it, that Pip was heartily glad when Herbert left them for the counting house.

"Us two being now alone, sir—" began Joe.

"Joe," Pip interrupted pettishly, "how can you call me sir?"

Joe looked at him with something like reproach, but with a sort of dignity, too. And then he went on to say that his chief reason for coming there to see Pip was to give him a message from Miss Havisham.

"Miss Havisham, Joe?" said Pip.

And Joe added that Miss Havisham had sent for him, and had asked him to tell Pip, when he next wrote, that Estella had come home, and would be glad to see him.

The blood rushed into Pip's face. And Joe rose from his chair.

"I have now concluded, sir," he said; "and, Pip, I wish you well, and ever prospering to a greater and greater heighth."

"But you are not going now, Joe?" said Pip.

"Yes, I am," said Joe.

"But you are coming back to dinner, Joe?"

"No, I am not," said Joe. And then he caught Pip by the hand. "Pip, dear old chap," said he, "life is made of ever so many partings welded together, as I may say, and one man's a blacksmith, and one's a goldsmith, and one's a coppersmith. Diwisions among such must come, and must be met as they come. You and me is not two figures to be together in London, Pip. I'm wrong out of the forge. You won't find half so much fault in me if you think of me in my forge dress, with my hammer in my hand. And supposing as you should ever wish to see me, you come and put your head in at the forge window, and see Joe the blacksmith there, at the old anvil, in the old burnt apron, sticking to the old work. And so God bless you, dear old Pip, old chap. God bless you!"

He kissed Pip gently on the forehead, and went out.

Pip and Herbert dine together

Pip was miserable and ashamed; and after thinking for a minute or two, he hurried after him to bring him back. But he could not find him in the neighbouring streets. Joe was gone.

9

Estella

Pip decided that he should go at once to his old town— not to see Joe, oh! no; but to see Estella; and went down the very next day by the afternoon coach; and on the way he built a beautiful castle in the air.

Miss Havisham had adopted Estella; she had as good as adopted him; and it could not fail to be her intention to bring them together now. Pip would restore the desolate house, admit the sunshine into the dark rooms, do all the brilliant deeds of the young knight of romance, and marry the princess.

He engaged a room at the Blue Boar, and early the next morning he started for Miss Havisham's. He rang the bell with an unsteady hand, and his heart began to beat so fast, that his breath came in short gasps.

"Oh!" said Sarah Pocket, admitting him. "You, is it, Mr Pip? You know your way, sir."

Yes, he knew it very well, for he had gone up the staircase in the dark many a time. And going up now, he tapped at the door of Miss Havisham's room.

"Pip's rap," he heard her say. "Come in, Pip."

She was in her chair near the old table, in the old bridal dress, with her two hands crossed on her stick. Sitting near her was an elegant lady whom Pip had never seen.

"How do you do, Pip?" said Miss Havisham. "So you kiss my hand as if I were a queen, eh? Well?"

"I heard, Miss Havisham," said Pip, "that you were so kind as to wish me to come and see you."

She repeated, "Well?"

The elegant lady lifted up her eyes and looked archly at Pip, and then he saw that the eyes were Estella's eyes. But she was so much changed, and was so much more beautiful, that as Pip looked at her, he felt himself to be the same coarse and common boy again.

She gave Pip her hand. And he stammered something about the pleasure he felt in seeing her again.

"Do you find her much changed, Pip?" asked Miss Havisham. "She was proud and insulting, and you wanted to go away from her. Do you remember?"

Pip said, with some confusion, that that was a long time ago. And Estella said, smiling, that she must have been very disagreeable.

"Is *he* changed?" Miss Havisham asked.

"Very much," said Estella, looking at him.

"Less coarse and common?" said Miss Havisham, playing with Estella's hair.

Estella laughed, and looked at Pip, and laughed again.

They sat in the darkened room where Pip had first seen her, and she said that she had just come from France, and that she was going to London. She seemed as proud and as wilful as of old. And oh! how much more beautiful she was!

It was settled that Pip should spend the rest of the day there, and return to the Blue Boar for the night, and to London the day after.

When they had talked for a while, Miss Havisham sent them both out to walk in the neglected garden. And soon they strayed to the spot where Pip had fought with the pale young gentleman.

"I must have been a singular little creature," said Estella, "to hide and see that fight that day; but I did, and I enjoyed it very much."

"You rewarded me very much," said Pip, thinking how she had let him kiss her cheek.

"Did I?" said Estella, as if she had forgotten all about it. "I remember that I did not like the boy you fought with."

"He and I are great friends now," said Pip.

"Are you?" And Estella added, "Since your change of fortune, you have changed your companions."

"Naturally," said Pip.

"And what was fit company for you once," said Estella, "would be quite unfit company for you now."

Pip thought of Joe. He had intended to go to the forge and see Joe. But he made up his mind now that it was unnecessary to see Joe.

Presently they found their way to the old brewery yard, and Pip reminded her where she had come out of the house, and given him his meat and drink that first day long ago.

"I do not remember," said Estella.

"Not remember that you made me cry?" asked Pip.

"No," said Estella. And she said it so carelessly that Pip felt that he could cry again at her indifference.

"You must know," said Estella, looking calmly at Pip, "that I have no softness in my heart—no—sympathy—feeling—nonsense."

And as she stood there, Pip had a curious idea that she reminded him of somebody he had lately seen. But who it was he could not tell.

"I am serious," said Estella. "If we are to be thrown much together, you had better believe it at once. No!" she added, imperiously stopping Pip as he was about to speak. "I have no tenderness for anyone or anything. Let us make one more round of the garden, and then go in."

They went round the ruined garden twice or thrice more, and then went back to the house; and there Pip heard, with surprise, that his guardian had come down to see Miss Havisham on business, and would come back to dinner.

Estella left him with Miss Havisham while she retired to change her dress, and Miss Havisham, beckoning Pip to come to her, whispered, "Is she beautiful, graceful, well-grown? Do you admire her, Pip!"

"Everybody must who sees her," answered Pip.

She put an arm round his neck, and drawing his head close down to hers, said, with passionate eagerness, "Love her, love her, love her! If she favours you, love her. If she tears your heart to pieces, love her ! Hear me, Pip! I adopted her to be loved. I made her into what she is, that she might be loved. Love her!"

But it was needless to tell Pip that; for he loved her already with all his heart. Then Miss Havisham let him go, and turning, Pip saw his guardian in the room.

"And so you are here, Pip?" he said.

"Miss Havisham wished me to come and see Estella," Pip replied.

"Well, Pip! How often have you seen Miss Estella before?"

"How often!" echoed Pip.

"Ah!" said Mr Jaggers. "Ten thousand times?"

"Oh!" said Pip. "Certainly not so many."

"Twice?"

"Jaggers," interrupted Miss Havisham, "leave my Pip alone, and go with him to your dinner."

So they groped their way down the dark stairs together; and Mr Jaggers and Pip had dinner with Miss Pocket and Estella; and were waited on by a maidservant whom Pip had never seen in all his comings and goings, but who, for anything he knew, had been in that mysterious house the whole time.

After dinner they played cards, and it was arranged that when Estella came to London, Pip should meet her at the coach. Then Mr Jaggers, who had also engaged a room at the Blue Boar, walked there with Pip.

They breakfasted together next morning, and travelling with Mr Jaggers in the same coach, Pip arrived safe in London—safe but not sound, for his heart was left with Estella.

He felt that he must tell all to his friend and chum. So he told Herbert that Estella had come back a most beautiful, most elegant creature; and added, "I love—I adore Estella."

"Lucky for you, then, Handel," said Herbert, "that you are picked out for her. Does Estella adore you?"

Pip shook his head gloomily. "Oh! She is thousands of miles away from me," he said.

One day, when Pip was busy with his books and Mr Pocket, he received a note from Estella, saying that she was coming to London by the midday coach the day after tomorrow, and that Miss Havisham wished him to meet her.

Pip began to haunt the coach office long before the coach was expected, but at last it rattled in, and he saw Estella's face at the window.

In her furred travelling dress, Estella seemed more delicately beautiful than she had ever seemed yet; and her manner was so winning that Pip wondered whether Miss Havisham had said anything to cause this change.

"I am going to Richmond," Estella said. "I am to have a carriage, and you are to take me. This is my purse, and you are to pay my charges out of it. Oh! You must take the purse! We have no choice—you and I—but to obey Miss Havisham."

"A carriage will have to be sent for, Estella," said Pip. "Will you rest here a little?"

"Yes," she answered. "I am to drink some tea, and you are to take care of me the while."

So Pip engaged a room and ordered tea, and thought he had never been so happy in all his life.

"Where are you going to Richmond?" he asked.

"I am going to live," said Estella, "at great expense with a lady there—a Mrs Brandley, who has the power of taking me

about and showing people to me, and showing me to people."
And then she added, "And how do you thrive with Mr Pocket?"

"As pleasantly as I could anywhere," replied Pip, "away from you."

"You silly boy!" said Estella. "How can you talk such nonsense?"

And as she looked round at him, Pip was again reminded, in a shadowy way, that she was like somebody he had lately seen.

And then the tea came in, and after that the carriage arrived, and they drove away to Richmond, and Pip left her there with Mrs Brandley.

Of course, Pip haunted the house at Richmond, and he often heard of Estella in London, for Estella had admirers by the dozen. There were picnics, parties, and plays, operas, concerts, and all sorts of pleasures, and Pip followed Estella everywhere.

But Pip was far more miserable than happy, for he was jealous of the other men that admired Estella.

10

Pip comes of Age

And now Pip began to contract expensive habits, and spent money
very lavishly—so lavishly, indeed, that he grew greatly in debt.
He and Startop joined a club called the Finches of the Grove; and
Herbert, of course, soon followed. And the Finches spent their
money very foolishly.

Bentley Drummle had left Mr Pocket's by this time, and he
also was a member of the club; but Pip did not like him any better.

Now Pip and Startop were rich young men, but Herbert had
nothing but the counting house. Pip would willingly have taken
Herbert's expenses on himself, but Herbert was proud and
would not allow Pip to help him, and he got into difficulties in
every direction.

It made Pip unhappy, and he began to feel that he had not
done Herbert good service by crowding his sparsely furnished
chambers with costly furniture, and leading him into expensive
ways of living.

"My dear Herbert, we are getting on badly," Pip would begin.

And Herbert would answer, "That was just what I was going
to say, my dear Handel."

"Then, Herbert, let us look into our affairs."

And then they would get out a pile of bills, and look over them, despondingly. And Herbert would say, "They are staring me out of countenance." And he would put them back into the drawer, and go out into the City to look about him.

One evening when they were looking over their bills in a very dejected fashion, the postman brought a letter for Pip.

"I hope there is nothing the matter," said Herbert, for the envelope was deeply edged with black.

The letter was from Trabb & Co., and it informed Pip that Mrs J. Gargery was dead, and that his attendance was requested at the funeral on Monday next.

Of course Pip went down to the old village, and when the funeral was over, and he had loitered about the forge with Joe, Pip slipped into the garden to have a talk with Biddy.

"I have not heard the particulars of my sister's death, Biddy," he said.

"She had been in one of her bad states," said Biddy, "for four days, when she came out of it towards evening," and said quite plainly, 'Joe.' As she had never said a word for a long time, I ran and fetched in Mr Gargery from the forge. She made signs to me that she wanted him to sit down close to her, and wanted me to put her arms round his neck. So I put her arms round his neck, and she laid her head down on his shoulder. Then she said 'Joe' again, and once, 'Pardon,' and once, 'Pip.' And then she died."

Biddy cried; and the tears came into Pip's eyes, too.

"I suppose you cannot remain here now, Biddy dear," he said.

"No," said Biddy. "I am going to try to get the place of mistress in the new school nearly finished here. But I hope Mrs Hubble and I shall be able to take some care of Mr Gargery, together, until he settles down."

"Of course I shall be often down here now," said Pip. "I am not going to leave poor Joe alone."

Biddy said never a word.

"Biddy, don't you hear me?" said Pip. "Why don't you speak?" he added impatiently.

"Are you quite sure, then, that you *will* come to see him often?" asked Biddy, looking at him with her clear and honest eyes.

Pip was angry that she doubted him, and he flung himself away, and he bade her good night very coldly as he went upstairs.

Early in the morning he was to go. And early in the morning he was out, and looking in at one of the windows of the forge. Joe was already there at work. "Goodbye, dear Joe!" he said. "No, don't wipe it off —for Heaven's sake give me your blackened hand!—I shall be down soon, Joe, and often."

"Never too soon, sir," said Joe. "And never too often, Pip."

"Biddy," said Pip, when he gave her his hand at parting, "I am not angry, but I am hurt."

And then he left them. But as he walked away, he felt in his heart that Biddy was quite right, and that he should *not* come back to see Joe.

Pip went from bad to worse in the way of increasing his debts; but he was to come of age very soon, and he and Herbert looked forward to his one-and-twentieth birthday with great expectations.

When the day came he received a note from Wemmick informing him that Mr Jaggers would be glad if he would call to see him in the afternoon. And when Pip arrived, Wemmick offered his congratulations in the outer office, and, at the same time, rubbed the side of his nose with a folded piece of tissue paper.

Pip went into his guardian's room. And Mr Jaggers said, "Well, Pip! I must call you Mr Pip today. Congratulations, Mr Pip. Take a chair, Mr Pip. Now, my young friend," said Mr Jaggers, "what do you suppose you are living at the rate of?"

"I fear I am quite unable to answer that question, sir," said Pip, abashed.

"I thought so!" said Mr Jaggers, blowing his nose. "Have you anything to ask me?"

"It would be a great relief to me to ask you several questions," said Pip.

"Ask one,' said Mr Jaggers.

"Is my benefactor to be made known to me today?"

"No. Ask another."

"Have—I—anything to receive, sir?"

"I thought we should come to it," said Mr Jaggers triumphantly. And he called to Wemmick to give him that piece of paper.

Wemmick appeared, handed in the paper with which he had been rubbing his nose, and disappeared.

"Now, Mr Pip," said Mr Jaggers, "attend, if you please. You have been drawing money pretty freely. Your name occurs pretty often in Wemmick's cashbook; but you are in debt, of course."

"I am afraid I must say yes, sir," answered Pip.

"Now, take this piece of paper in your hand. Unfold it. And tell me what it is."

"This is a bank note," said Pip "for five hundred pounds."

"And a very handsome sum of money, too," said Mr Jaggers. "That handsome sum of money, Pip, is your own. It is a present to you today, in earnest of your expectations. And at the rate of five hundred pounds a year you are to live, until the giver of the whole appears. That is to say, you will now take your money affairs into your own hands, and you will draw from Wemmick one hundred and twenty-five pounds per quarter."

Pip was beginning to say how liberal his unknown benefactor was, when Mr Jaggers stopped him. "I am not paid, Pip," he said coolly, "to carry your words to anyone."

"Is it likely," began Pip, "that my benefactor will soon—"

"Will soon what?" said Mr Jaggers.

"—Will soon come to London? Or summon me anywhere else?"

"That's a question I must not be asked," said Mr Jaggers. 'When your benefactor is known, you and your benefactor will settle your own affairs. And that's all I have got to say."

Pip left him, and went into the outer office to talk to Wemmick. For the fact was that when the five hundred pounds had come into his pocket, the thought had come into his head that he might be able to help Herbert, and it appeared to him that Wemmick would be able to advise him.

"Mr Wemmick," said Pip, "I am very desirous to help a friend. This friend is trying to get on in a commercial life, but has no money. Now, I want to help him to make a beginning."

"With money down?" said Wemmick.

"With *some* money down," said Pip, thinking uneasily of the debts he had to pay.

Wemmick had been a good friend to Pip, and he hastily arranged that Pip should go to his little place at Walworth, where they could talk the matter over in private.

At Walworth, Pip told him that it was Herbert he wanted to help, but that Herbert must never suspect that Pip had had a hand in helping him.

And Wemmick arranged the whole affair so cleverly that in a week's time he found a worthy young merchant named Clarriker, not long established in business, who wanted intelligent help, and who wanted capital—or money down—and who, in due time, would want a partner.

Between him and Pip secret articles were signed, of which Herbert was the subject; and Pip paid the merchant half of his five hundred pounds down, and engaged to pay other payments at certain dates, out of his income.

And one afternoon Herbert came home with a radiant face, and with a mighty piece of news for Pip. It was that he had fallen in with a young merchant named Clarriker, who had taken an extraordinary liking for him, and that he believed the opening had come at last.

The opening came indeed. Herbert entered Clarriker's House; and he was so happy telling Pip about it, that Pip could scarcely keep the tears out of his eyes.

And when Pip went to bed that night, he really did cry in earnest to think that his expectations had done some good to somebody; for what with his debts, and what with his misery at Estella's coldness, Pip had begun to think that it would have been better for him if he had never had any expectations at all, and that he had been left to work in the old forge with Joe.

"Pip," said Estella, one evening when they sat together by the window of the house at Richmond, "will you never take warning?"

"Warning of what?" asked Pip.

"Of me."

"Warning not to be attracted by you, do you mean, Estella?"

"Do I mean," retorted Estella. "If you do not know what I mean, you are blind."

Pip wanted to tell her that love is blind; but he felt that it was ungenerous to press his love upon her, when she knew that she could not choose but obey Miss Havisham. And that Miss Havisham had chosen him for Estella's husband, Pip was as sure as that he loved Estella with all his heart.

"At any rate," said Pip, "I have no warning given me just now, for you wrote to me to come to you this time."

"That's true," said Estella, and she smiled her cold, careless smile. "Miss Havisham wishes to have me for a day at Satis House. You are to take me there, and bring me back, if you will."

So they went down the next day but one, and found Miss Havisham in the old candle-lighted room. And it seemed to Pip almost dreadful to see the weird, eager way in which she hung upon Estella's beauty, as if she were devouring the beautiful creature she had reared.

And, then, from Estella she would look at Pip, with a searching glance, saying, in a witchlike whisper, "How does she use you, Pip? How does she use you?"

They slept that night at Satis House, and on the next day returned to London. And a few days later, what was Pip's indignation when he went to the club, to hear Bentley Drummle toasting *Estella*!

"Estella who?" cried Pip.

"Never you mind," retorted Drummle.

"Estella of where?" persisted Pip. "You are bound to say of where."

"Of Richmond, gentlemen," said Drummle, addressing the other Finches of the Grove. "And a peerless beauty!"

And though Pip knew him to be a clumsy, sulky boorish fellow, Pip was more jealous than ever.

And soon he found out, not only that Drummle had begun to follow Estella everywhere, but that she allowed him to do it. And Pip determined to speak to her.

They were at an Assembly Ball at Richmond; and Estella was waiting for Mrs Brandley to take her home. Pip was with her, for he almost always accompanied them to and fro from such places.

"Estella," he said, "that fellow Drummle is looking from that corner yonder over at us. He has been hovering about you all night."

"Moths and all sorts of ugly creatures," replied Estella, "hover about a lighted candle."

"It makes me wretched, Estella, that you should encourage a

man like Drummle—an ill-tempered, lowering, stupid fellow. You know he has nothing to recommend him but a great deal of money, and a long roll of ancestors."

"Don't be wretched, Pip," returned Estella. "It's not worth talking about."

"Yes, it is," said Pip. "I cannot bear that people should say, 'She throws away her graces and affections on a mere boor.' I have seen you give him looks and smiles this very night, such as you never give to—me."

"Do you want me, then," said Estella, turning suddenly, with a fixed and serious look, "to deceive and entrap you?"

"Do you deceive and entrap him, Estella?"

"Yes, and many others—all of them," said Estella "but you. Here is Mrs Brandley. I'll say no more."

11

Pip wakes from his Dream

Two years passed away. Pip was twenty-three years of age. And the name of his benefactor had not yet been disclosed to him.

Herbert and he had left Barnard's Inn, and now lived in the Temple, their chambers being in Garden Court, down by the river.

Pip had left off studying with Mr Pocket, but he had a great taste for reading, and he read regularly so many hours a day.

Herbert was doing very well at Clarriker's, and business having taken Herbert on a journey to France, Pip was alone, and feeling rather dispirited.

The night was wet and stormy, and Pip was reading, with his watch upon the table, when St Paul's and all the many church clocks in the City struck eleven, and as the sound died away, he heard a footstep on the stairs.

Remembering that the staircase lights were blown out, Pip took up his reading lamp, and went out to the stairhead. Whoever was below had stopped on seeing his lamp, for all was quiet.

"There is someone there, is there not?" Pip called out, looking down.

"Yes," said the voice from the darkness beneath.

"What floor do you want?" asked Pip.

"The top. Mr Pip."

"That is my name," said Pip. "There is nothing the matter?"

"Nothing the matter," answered the voice. And the man came on.

Pip stood with his lamp held out over the stair rail, and as he came slowly within its light, Pip saw a face that was strange to him, looking up with a curious air of pleasure at the sight of him.

Pip saw that he was roughly dressed, like a voyager by sea; that he had long iron-grey hair; and that he was browned and hardened by exposure to the weather. And, as he ascended the last stair or two, Pip saw, with a stupid kind of amazement, that he was holding out both his hands to him.

"Pray, what is your business?" asked Pip.

"My business?" the man repeated, pausing. "Ah! Yes. I will explain my business, by your leave."

"Do you wish to come in?" said Pip.

"Yes," he replied. "I wish to come in, master."

Pip took him into the room he had just left, and the man, looking about him with an air of wondering pleasure, as if he had some part in the things he admired, pulled off a rough outer coat and his hat. Then Pip saw that his head was furrowed and bald. And that the long iron-grey hair grew only on its sides. And once more he saw him holding out his hands to him.

"What do you mean?" asked Pip.

"It's disappointing to a man," he said, in a coarse, broken voice, "arter having looked for'ard so distant, and come so fur;

but you're not to blame for that. Give me half a minute, please." And sitting down and looking over his shoulder, he added, "There is no one nigh. Is there?"

"Why do you, a stranger coming into my rooms at this time of night, ask that question?" said Pip. And he was about to lay hold of the man to turn him out, when suddenly he knew him—knew him for the convict he had met in the old churchyard long ago!

There was no need to take a file from his pocket, and show it to Pip. No need to take his handkerchief from his neck and twist it round his head, and hugging himself with both his arms, take a shivering turn across the room, looking back at him for recognition. Pip knew him well.

He came back to where Pip stood, and again held out both his hands. Reluctantly Pip let him take his own. And grasping them heartily, the man raised them to his lips, kissed them, and still held them.

"You acted noble, my boy," said he. "Noble, Pip. And I have never forgot it."

He looked as if he were going to embrace Pip, and Pip, laying a hand upon his breast, put him away. "Stay," said he. "Keep off! If you are grateful to me for what I did when I was a little child, I hope you have shown your gratitude by mending your way of life. But surely you must understand that I cannot wish to have anything more to do with you now."

He looked at Pip with such a singular, fixed look that Pip added hurriedly, "But you are wet, and you look weary. Will you drink something before you go?"

He had replaced his neckerchief loosely, and biting a long

end of it, and still looking at Pip, he said, "I think I *will* drink afore I go."

There was a tray ready on the side table, and Pip made him some hot rum and water. And when he pushed the glass to him, he saw, with amazement, that the convict's eyes were full of tears.

"I hope," said Pip, "that you will not think I spoke harshly to you just now. I had no intention of doing it."

The man again stretched out his hand. Pip gave him his own. Then he drank, and drew his sleeve across his eyes.

"How are you living?" asked Pip.

"I've been a sheep farmer and a stockbreeder, away in the New World," said he.

"I hope you have done well?" said Pip.

"I've done wonderful well. There's others went out alonger me, as has done well too, but no man has done nigh as well as me. I'm famous for it."

"I'm glad to hear it," answered Pip.

"And may I ask how *you* have done well since you and me was out on them lone, shivering marshes?" He emptied his glass, got up, and stood at the side of the fire, with his heavy, brown hand on the mantelshelf, and looked steadily at Pip.

Pip suddenly began to tremble, and stammered out, that he was chosen to succeed to some property.

"Might a mere warmint ask what property?" said he.

"I don't know," faltered Pip.

"Might a mere warmint ask whose property?"

Again Pip faltered, "I don't know."

"Could I make a guess, I wonder," said the convict, "at your income since you came of age? As to the first figure, now. Five?"

With his heart beating like a sledgehammer, Pip rose out of his chair, looking wildly at him.

"Concerning a guardian," went on the man. "Some lawyer, may be. As to the first letter of that lawyer's name, now. Would it be J?"

As the truth came flashing upon Pip, he seemed to struggle for every breath he drew.

"Put it," went on the convict, "as the employer of that lawyer—whose name might be Jaggers—had come over sea to Portsmouth, and had landed there, and wanted to come on to you. Why I wrote from Portsmouth to a person in London for particulars of your address. That person's name? Why, Wemmick."

Pip could not speak a word. He stood with a hand on the chair back, looking fearfully at the convict, and he grew so faint that he would have fallen had not the man caught him, drew him to the sofa, put him against the cushions, and bent on one knee before him.

"Yes, Pip, dear boy, I've made a gentleman of you," he said. "It's me wot has done it! I swore sure as ever I spec'lated and got rich, you should get rich. I lived rough, that you might live smooth. That there hunted, dunghill dog, wot you kep' life in, got his head so high that he could make a gentleman—and, Pip, you're him!"

Pip felt such a horror of him that he shrank from him as if he had been some terrible beast; but, in his joy and triumph, the convict did not notice it.

"Look'ee here, Pip. I'm your second father. You're my son—more to me nor any son. I've put away money, only for you to spend. 'May I be struck dead,' I says, 'but wot, if I gets liberty and money, I'll make that boy a gentleman!' And I done it! Why, look at you, dear boy. Look at these here lodgings of yourn—fit for a lord! Look at your linen—fine and beautiful! Look at your clothes—better ain't to be got!"

Again he took both Pip's hands, and put them to his lips, while Pip's blood ran cold within him.

"Don't you mind talking, Pip," said he, drawing his sleeve over his eyes, with the old click in his throat that Pip well remembered. "You ain't looked slowly forward to this as I have, dear boy. You wosn't prepared for this as I wos. But didn't you never think it might be me?"

"Oh no, no, no!" Pip answered at last. "Never, never!"

"Well, you see it wos me, and single-handed. Never a soul in it but my own self and Mr Jaggers. When I was a hired-out shepherd in a solitary hut, I got money from my master which died, and got my liberty and went for myself."

For in those days, convicts were sent out to Botany Bay, in Australia, where they were hired out on farms, to work without wages, for a certain number of years.

"In everything I went for," added the man, "I went for you. It all prospered wonderful. And it was a recompense to me, dear boy, to know, in secret, that I was making a gentleman. This way I kep' myself a-going. And this way I held steady before my mind, that I would for certain come one day and see my boy, and make myself known to him. It warn't easy, Pip, for me to leave them parts, nor yet it warn't safe. But I done it at last. Dear boy, I done it! Where will you put me?" he asked.

"To sleep?" asked Pip. And he added, rising from the sofa, "My friend is absent. You must have his room."

"He won't come back tomorrow, will he?"

"No," said Pip, speaking as if he were in a dream.

"Because," and he dropped his voice, "look'ee here, dear boy, caution is necessary."

"How do you mean?" said Pip. "Caution?"

"By Heaven, it's death! I was sent for life. It's death to come back to England. And I should of a certainty be hanged if took."

Pip—still as if he were in a dream—closed the shutters, and then closed and made fast the doors. Then he took him into Herbert's room, and left him.

Returning to the chamber where they had talked together, Pip mended the fire, and sat down by it, afraid to go to bed, thinking, in a stunned way, how the beautiful castle he had been building in the air had tumbled to pieces.

Miss Havisham's intentions towards him were mere dreams of his own. Estella was not designed for him. Miss Havisham had had nothing to do with making his fortune at all. All—all had been done by the convict!

In every gust of wind Pip imagined he heard pursuers Twice he could have sworn there was a knocking and whispering at the outer door. And he remembered that he had seen him, with his childish eyes, to be a desperately violent man; that he had heard that other convict, with whom he had fought in the ditch, say, over and over again, that he had tried to murder him.

Perhaps it might not be safe to be shut up there with him in the dead of the lonely night. And Pip, taking a candle, crept softly into Herbert's room.

He had rolled a handkerchief round his head, and was fast asleep, and quietly too, though he had a pistol lying on his pillow. And gently removing the key to the outside of his door, Pip turned it on him before he again sat down by the fire.

First of all he must secure the safety of his dreaded visitor; and he was thankful that the boy in top-boots was not in his service now. An old laundress and her niece attended to his rooms; and when they arrived, Pip told them that his uncle had come in the night, and was then asleep.

Then he washed and dressed, and, still in a sort of dream, he found himself sitting by the fire again, waiting for the convict to come to breakfast. By and by his door opened, and he came out. Pip thought he looked worse by daylight.

"I have given out," said Pip softly, "that you are my uncle."

"That's it, dear boy! Call me uncle." And he added, "I took the name of Provis on board ship."

"What is your real name?" asked Pip.

"Magwitch," he whispered. "Chris'ened Abel."

"Are you known in London?"

"I hope not!"

"Were you—tried—in London?"

He nodded. "First knowed Mr Jaggers that way. Jaggers was for me." And sitting down, and taking from his pocket a great horn-handled knife with which he cut his food, he began to eat ravenously.

"And this is the gentleman wot I made!" he said, when he had finished. "It does me good fur to look at you. My gentleman must have horses, Pip. Horses to ride and horses to drive. There mustn't be no mud on *his* boots." And bringing a great, thick pocketbook, bursting with papers, out of his coat, he tossed it on the table.

"There's something worth spending in that there book, dear boy. It's yourn. All I've got ain't mine. It's yourn. And there's more where that came from, Pip."

"Stop!" said Pip, almost in a frenzy of fear. "I want to know how you are to be kept out of danger—how long you are going to stay."

"Well, dear boy, the danger ain't so great, without I was informed agen. There's Jaggers, and there's Wemmick, and there's you. Who else is there to inform?"

"Is there no chance person who might know you in the street?"

"Well," he returned, "there ain't many. Nor yet I don't intend to advertise myself in the newspapers by the name of A.M. come back from Botany Bay."

"And how long do you remain?" asked Pip.

"How long?" His jaw dropped as he stared at Pip. "I'm not a-going back, dear boy. I've come for good."

"Where will you live?" said the wretched Pip. "What is to be done with you?"

"Dear boy," he returned, "there's disguising wigs can be bought for money, and there's spectacles, and black clothes; others has done it safe afore; and what others has done afore, others can do agen."

It appeared to Pip that he could do no better than secure him some quiet lodging hard by, of which he might take possession when Herbert returned, and Herbert was expected in a few days. The secret must be confided to Herbert. And Pip told the convict so.

"Dear boy," said he, pulling a greasy little black Bible out of his pocket, "we'll have him on his oath first."

Pip now suggested that Provis—as he intended to call him—should wear a dress like a prosperous farmer's, and while Pip went out to purchase the clothes, Provis was to remain shut up in the chambers, and was on no account to open the door.

Pip knew of a respectable lodging house in Essex Street, the back of which looked into the Temple, and going there first, he secured the top floor for his uncle, Mr Provis. He then ordered the clothes required from different tradesmen, and that business finished, he found his way to Little Britain.

Mr Jaggers was at his desk, but seeing Pip enter, he got up immediately and stood before him.

"Now Pip, be careful," he said. "Don't tell me anything. I don't want to know anything. I am not curious."

And Pip saw that he knew the man was come.

"I merely want, Mr Jaggers," said Pip, "to make sure what I have been told is true. I have been informed, by a person named Abel Magwitch, that he is the benefactor so long unknown to me."

"That is the man," said Mr Jaggers.

"I cannot blame you for my mistakes, sir," said the wretched Pip, "but I always supposed it was Miss Havisham."

"As you say, Pip," returned Mr Jaggers coolly, "I am not to blame for that."

"And yet it looked so like it, sir," pleaded Pip.

"Not a particle of proof, Pip," said Mr Jaggers. "Take nothing on its looks."

"I have no more to say," said the miserable Pip.

"I cautioned Magwitch," said Mr Jaggers, "when he wrote to me from Australia, hinting that he wanted to see you in England, that I must hear no more of that; that he was not at all likely to obtain a pardon; that his returning to this country would be an act of felony. Good day, Pip," and he held out his hand.

Pip went back to his chambers, and the next day the clothes he had ordered came home, and Provis put them on. But to Pip's thinking, he still looked like the slouching fugitive on the marshes; that from head to foot there was Convict in the very grain of the man. And the more Provis admired him, and the fonder he was of Pip, the more did the unhappy Pip shudder from him.

12

The Convict's Story

Five days passed, and then one evening when dinner was over, Pip heard Herbert's foot upon the stairs. Provis, who had been dozing, staggered up from the chair, and in an instant Pip saw his jackknife shining in his hand.

"Quiet!" said Pip. "It's only Herbert!" And Herbert burst in, with an air of breezy cheerfulness.

"Handel, my dear fellow, how are you?" he cried. "Why, Handel, you've grown quite pale and thin! Handel, my—Hulloa! I beg your pardon." And he stopped and looked at Provis.

Provis, regarding him with fixed attention, was slowly putting up his jackknife, and groping in another pocket for something else.

"Herbert," said Pip, quickly shutting the double doors, "something very strange has happened. This is—a visitor of mine."

And Provis, coming forward with his little black Bible, addressed himself to the newcomer. "Take it in your right hand," he said. "Heaven strike you dead if ever you split in any way sumever. Kiss it."

"Do so, as he wishes it," Pip said to Herbert.

And Herbert complying, with a look of amazement, Provis immediately shook hands with him. "Now, you're on your oath," he said.

It is impossible to describe the astonishment and uneasiness of Herbert when Pip recounted the whole of the secret; and Pip saw, in Herbert's face, that he, too, shrank from the man, and how anxious he seemed to get Provis away to his lodging, that he and Pip could talk alone together.

At midnight Pip took him round to Essex Street, and saw him safely in at his own door, and returned as fast as he could to Herbert.

Herbert received him with open arms, and Pip felt what a blessed thing it was to have a friend. "What is to be done, Herbert?" he said. "What is to be done?"

"My poor dear Handel," said Herbert, "I am too much stunned to think."

"Herbert, something *must* be done. He wants me to spend more money—he talks of horses and carriages, and other luxuries. He must be stopped."

"You mean that you cannot accept anything more from him?"

"How can I?" Pip cried. "Think of him. Look at him. And yet the dreadful truth is, Herbert, that he is strongly attached to me. Was there ever such a fate!"

"My poor dear Handel!" repeated Herbert.

"And, Herbert, I am heavily in debt—very heavily for me

who have no expectations—and I have been bred to no calling. I am fit for nothing. I am only fit to go for a soldier."

"Soldiering won't do," said Herbert. "That is absurd. You would be much better in Clarriker's house. I am working up towards a partnership, you know."

Poor Herbert! He little suspected with whose money!

"But there is another question, Handel," went on Herbert. "This is a desperate, determined man, who has long had one fixed idea. If after all his toil and waiting, you should now forsake him, you will make his gains worthless to him; and in his despair, he may put himself into the way of being taken, and—hanged."

Pip was so struck with the horror of this idea that he could not rest in his chair, and began walking to and fro.

"The first and chief thing to be done," said Herbert, "is to get him out of England. You will have to go with him. He will never go without you. Are you sure that you can take no further benefits from him? Are you fully convinced that you must break with him?"

"Oh! Herbert, can you ask me?" exclaimed Pip.

"Then you must get him out of England before you stir a finger in breaking with him. That done, break with him, in Heaven's name, and we'll see it out together."

They shook hands upon it, and Pip felt a little comforted. And it was agreed that, as they knew nothing of the man's history, Pip should ask Provis about it at breakfast next morning.

He came round at the appointed time, full of plans "for his gentleman's coming out strong, and like a gentleman."

And Pip said, "I have told my friend of your struggle with that other man, when the soldiers found you on the marshes. We want to know something about that man—and about you."

"Well!" said Provis, "you are on your oath, you know, Pip's comrade?"

"Assuredly," replied Herbert.

And, after a little consideration, Provis began:

"Dear boy, and Pip's comrade, I've no more notion where I was born than you have. The first thing I remember is a-thieving turnips for my living. I knowed my name to be Magwitch, chris'ened Abel, and there wasn't a soul that see young Abel Magwitch but either drove him off, or took him up. A bit of a poacher, a bit of a labourer, a bit of a hawker, in jail and out of jail, I got to be a man.

"At Epsom Races, a matter of twenty year ago, I got acquainted wi' a man whose skull I'd crack wi' this poker, if I get it on this hob. His right name was Compeyson. And that's the man, dear boy, what you see me a-pounding in the ditch.

"He set up fur a gentleman, this Compeyson, and had learning. He was good-looking too, and was a smooth one to talk. 'This is a man that might suit you,' says a fellow to him, the night afore the great race—meaning I was.

"'What can you do?' says Compeyson.

"'Eat and drink,' I says.

"Compeyson laughed, looked at me very noticing, giv' me five shillings, and appointed me to meet him next night. I went to Compeyson next night, and he took me on to be his man and pardner. And Compeyson's business, in which we was to go

"There is no one nigh, is there?"

pardners, was the swindling, handwriting forging, stolen banknote passing, and suchlike. All sorts of traps as Compeyson could set and get the profits from, and let another man in for— that was Compeyson's business.

"There was another in with Compeyson, as was called Arthur. Him and Compeyson had been in a bad thing with a rich lady some years afore, and they'd made a pot of money by it; but Compeyson betted and gamed, and he'd have run through the King's taxes.

"Then Arthur died, but Compeyson took it easy, and him and me were very busy. It 'ud take a week to go into the things that Compeyson planned, and I done. I'll simply say to you, dear boy and Pip's comrade, that that man got me into such nets, as made me his black slave. He was younger than me, but he had learning, and over-matched me five hundred times. My missis—Stop, though, I ain't brought *her* in—"

He looked about in a confused way, and turned his face to the fire.

"Well, at last, me and Compeyson was both taken upon a charge of putting stolen notes in circulation. And I was so miserable poor that I sold my clothes afore I could get Jaggers. When we was put in the dock, I noticed what a gentleman Compeyson looked, and what a common sort of wretch *I* looked.

"And when it came to character, wasn't it Compeyson as had been known by witnesses in clubs and societies? And wasn't it me as had been knowed up hill and down dale in lockups?

"And when the verdict came, warn't it Compeyson as was recommended to mercy for giving up all the information he could agen me? And when we were sentenced, ain't it him that gets seven year, and me fourteen? 'Once out of this court,' says I, 'I'll smash that face o' yourn!'

"We was in the same prison ship, but I couldn't get at him for long. At last I come behind him, and hit him on the cheek, and got put into the black hole.

"The black hole of that ship weren't a strong one. I escaped to the shore, and I was a-hiding among the graves there when I first see my boy." And he looked at Pip with the greatest affection.

"By my boy I was giv' to understand as Compeyson had also escaped, and was out on them marshes. I hunted him down. I smashed his face. And I swore I'd drag him back to prison, and held him tight till the soldiers came.

"I was put in irons, brought to trial agen, and sent to Botany Bay for life. I didn't stop for life, dear boy and Pip's comrade, being here."

"Is Compeyson dead?" Pip asked after a silence.

"He hopes *I* am, if he's alive," answered Provis, with a fierce look.

Herbert had been writing with his pencil in a book. He softly pushed the book over to Pip. And, as Provis sat with his eyes on the fire, Pip read these words:

"Young Havisham's name was Arthur. Compeyson is the man who professed to be Miss Havisham's lover."

And now a new fear took hold of Pip. If Compeyson were alive and should discover Provis's return, would he hesitate to release himself from a dreaded enemy by becoming an informer? That Compeyson stood in mortal fear of him, Pip could not doubt. Provis must be taken out of England without delay.

"Before I go abroad with him," Pip said to Herbert, "I must see Miss Havisham and Estella."

He called at Richmond, and learned from Mrs Brandley that Estella had gone down to Satis House And it was arranged that while Pip was away for one night, Herbert should take charge of Provis.

The coach stopped as usual at the Blue Boar, and whom should Pip see coming out in the drizzling rain to look at the coach—but Bentley Drummle!

"Beastly place, this!" said Drummle. "Your part of the country, I think?" And then he called out to the waiter, with a look of triumph at Pip, "I say, waiter! The lady won't ride today. The weather won't do. I'll dine at the young lady's this evening."

Angry and miserable, Pip went his way to Satis House; and in the room where the dressing table stood, he found Miss Havisham and Estella.

"Miss Havisham," said Pip, "I am as unhappy as you can ever have meant me to be."

Miss Havisham seemed rather confused, but she looked steadily at Pip.

"I have found out who my benefactor is. It is not a fortunate discovery, and is not likely to enrich me in station or fortune. More I must not say. It is not my secret, but another's. And when I fell into the mistake I have so long remained in, you led me on. Miss Havisham, was that kind?"

"Who am I," said Miss Havisham, striking her stick against the floor, "who am I that I should be kind? You made your own mistakes. I never made them."

And then, in a burst, Pip told her that she had encouraged his mistake to punish her greedy relations, who thought Miss Havisham was going to leave her money to him.

He said, too, that of all her relations only Mr Pocket and Herbert were incapable of doing anything mean. And he told her what he had done to help Herbert to a partnership with Clarriker; how Herbert knew nothing about it; and how nine hundred pounds was still needed to complete the affair; and that it was impossible now for him to do anything more for Herbert.

"Miss Havisham," added Pip, "will you spare the money to do my friend a lasting service in life?"

She said nothing, but, withdrawing her eyes from Pip, looked steadily into the fire.

"Estella," said Pip, "you know that I have loved you dearly. I should have said this sooner, but for my long mistake. I thought Miss Havisham meant us for one another."

"I have tried to warn you not to love me," said Estella. "Have I not, Pip?"

Pip said in a miserable manner, "Yes."

"But you would not be warned," said Estella.

"Is it not true," said Pip, "that Bentley Drummle is in the town, and that he dines with you today? You would never marry him, Estella?"

She looked first at Miss Havisham, and then she said, "I am going to be married to him."

Pip dropped his head into his hands, and when he raised it again, there was a ghastly look upon Miss Havisham's face, and she put her hand to her heart and held it there, staring at Pip with pity and remorse.

"This will pass in time," said Estella. "You will get me out of your thoughts in a week."

"Never, Estella. You are part of myself," answered Pip. "You have been in my thoughts ever since I first came here—the rough, common boy whose poor heart you wounded even then. Oh, God bless you! God forgive you!" And holding her hand for a moment to his lips, he left her.

He had such a horror of meeting Bentley Drummle at the Blue Boar that he started off to walk all the way to London. And it was past midnight when he crossed London Bridge.

His nearest way to the Temple was close to the riverside through Whitefriars. He was not expected till tomorrow, but he had his keys, and could get in without disturbing Herbert.

There was a gate leading from Whitefriars to the Temple, and here the night porter looked at him very attentively. So Pip mentioned his name as he passed.

"I thought so," said the porter. "Here's a note, sir. The messenger that brought it said would you be so good as to read it by my lantern?"

Much surprised by this request, Pip took the note, and opened it. The watchman held up his light, and Pip read in Wemmick's writing:—

"DON'T GO HOME."

13

In Hiding

Turning from the Temple gate, Pip made his way to Fleet Street, and engaged a room at a place he knew near Covent Garden, and early next morning he made his way to Walworth to see Wemmick.

"Halloa, Mr Pip!" said Wemmick. "You did come home, then?"

"Yes," returned Pip. "But I didn't go home."

"That's all right," said Wemmick. And then he told Pip that he had learned that there was some suspicion about a returned convict from Botany Bay, and that Pip had been watched at his chambers in the Temple, and might be watched again.

"By whom?" inquired Pip.

"I would not go into that," said Wemmick. "I heard it as I have, in my time, heard many curious things."

"You have heard of a man of bad character," said Pip, "whose true name is Compeyson?"

Wemmick nodded.

"Is he in London?"

Wemmick nodded again. And then he told Pip that after hearing what he had heard, he had gone to the chambers at the Temple to speak to him, and not finding him there, he had gone to Clarriker's to find Herbert, and gave Herbert to understand that while Pip was out of the way, he had better get Provis out of the way; and that Herbert, greatly alarmed, had taken the convict to a lodging by the riverside between Limehouse and Greenwich.

"It would be a handy spot," said Wemmick, "to slip him on board a foreign boat as soon as it is prudent; and I'll look about and tell you when it is prudent. Here is the address. And now, Mr Pip, there can be no harm in your going there tonight, and seeing for yourself that all is well, *before you go home*. But after you have gone home, don't go back there." And he advised Pip to stop at his house at Walworth all day, and go to Provis after dark.

Eight o'clock had struck that evening when Pip found his way to Mill-Pond Bank, as the place near Greenwich was called, and his knock was answered by a pleasant, elderly woman. But Herbert was just behind her, and he silently led Pip into the parlour.

"All is well, Handel," whispered Herbert. "And he is quite satisfied, though eager to see you." And he took Pip to the top of the house where Provis was comfortably settled.

The convict did not appear alarmed, but it struck Pip that he was strangely softened. And when Herbert and he sat down with him by the fire, he asked Provis whether he relied on Wemmick's judgment.

"Ay, ay, dear boy!" he answered, with a grave nod. "Jaggers knows."

"I have talked with Wemmick," said Pip, "and have come to tell you what caution he gave me, and what advice."

And then, without mentioning Compeyson's name, Pip told him how Wemmick had heard that his chambers had been watched; how Wemmick had advised Provis's keeping close for a time, and Pip's keeping away from him, till they could get him on board some foreign ship.

"I will go with you," said Pip, "or follow close upon you, whichever Wemmick thinks best."

The convict listened quietly. His coming back was a venture, he said, and he had always known it to be a venture. He had very little fear of his safety with such good help.

Then Herbert spoke. "We are both good watermen, Handel," he said, "and could take him down the river ourselves when the right time comes. No boat would then be hired for the purpose, and no boatmen. Don't you think it might be a good thing if you began at once to keep a boat at the Temple stairs, and were in the habit of rowing up and down the river? You fall into that habit, and then who notices or minds?"

Pip liked this scheme. And Provis was quite elated by it. And it was arranged that if Pip rowed past Mill-Pond Bank, Provis should take no notice of him whatever. Also that he should pull down the blind in his east window whenever he saw Pip's boat, as a signal that all was well.

Pip then rose to go. "I don't like leaving you here," he said, "though I cannot doubt your being safer here than near me. Goodbye!"

"Dear boy," said the convict, clasping Pip's hands, "I don't know when we may meet again, and I don't like goodbye. Say Good night!"

"Good night!" said Pip. "Herbert will go regularly between us, and when the time comes, you may be certain I shall be ready."

Some weeks passed without bringing any change. They waited for Wemmick. But Wemmick made no sign. And Pip rowed in his own boat up and down the river.

It was an unhappy life he lived—always anxious for Provis, and greatly oppressed at the thought that Estella must now be married.

One afternoon, late in the month of February, Pip came ashore at the wharf at dusk. He had pulled down as far as Greenwich, and both in coming and going, he had seen the blind in the convict's window down—the signal, All well.

Pip felt depressed, and instead of going home to his chambers at the Temple, he had dinner at a chop house by the riverside, and made up his mind to go to a theatre close by. And when the play was over, and Pip came out, who should be waiting for him near the door but Mr Wopsle.

"I saw you, Mr Pip," he said, as Pip shook hands. "But who else was at the Play? It is the strangest thing," added Mr Wopsle, "but I could have sworn to him."

"Sworn to whom?" asked Pip, feeling suddenly alarmed.

"You remember in old times, Mr Pip, a certain Christmas Day when you were a child, that there was a chase after two convicts, and that we joined in it, and Gargery took you on his back?"

"I remember it well," said Pip.

"And you remember that we came up with the two in a ditch, and that there was a scuffle between them, and that one of them had been much mauled about the face by the other?"

"I see it all before me," answered Pip.

"Then, Mr Pip, one of those two prisoners sat behind you to-night."

Pip tried hard to keep himself calm. And then he said, "Which of the two do you suppose you saw?"

"The one that had been mauled," answered Mr Wopsle readily.

"This is very curious," said Pip, speaking as if it were nothing at all to him. And then he got rid of Mr Wopsle. But the terror he felt at Compeyson's having been behind him, like a ghost, followed him all the way home.

Compeyson had seldom been out of his thoughts since the hiding had begun. And to think that he had been so unconscious of his presence after all his care! That Compeyson had been actually at his elbow!

He found Herbert in when he got home, and they held a very serious council by the fire. But there was nothing to be done, saving to write to tell Wemmick what he had that night found out, and to remind him that they were still waiting for his signal.

Still Wemmick gave no sign. And then Mr Jaggers invited Pip to dinner. Wemmick had been invited too.

"Here's a note from Miss Havisham, Pip," said Mr Jaggers. "She tells me that she wants to see you on a little matter of business."

Pip looked at Wemmick. He seemed to say, "Go." So Pip said, "I'll go at once."

Then the housekeeper came in with another dish, and Mr Jaggers kept her for a moment or two. And as she stood listening, and looking at him intently, Pip thought, surely he had seen eyes like hers before.

He looked at those eyes, and he looked at that flowing hair, and comparing them with other eyes and other hair that he knew well, he suddenly felt absolutely certain that this woman was Estella's mother.

Only twice more did the housekeeper reappear, and then her stay in the room was very short. But her hands were Estella's hands, and her eyes were Estella's eyes, and if she had reappeared a hundred times, Pip could not have been surer than he now was that she was the mother of Estella.

Pip took his leave early, and Wemmick left with him, and when they got out of the house, Pip asked him if he had ever seen Miss Havisham's adopted daughter.

"No," said Wemmick.

"Wemmick," said Pip, 'before I first went to Mr Jaggers's private house, you told me to notice that housekeeper. A wild beast tamed, you called her. How did Mr Jaggers tame her?"

"That's his secret," answered Wemmick. "She has been with him many a long year."

"I wish you would tell me her story," said Pip. "I have a particular interest in knowing it."

"Twenty years ago," said Wemmick, "that woman was tried at the Old Bailey for murder, and was acquitted." And he went on to say she was a very handsome young woman, and had been married to a tramping man, and was a perfect fury for jealousy. That she had a child some three years old, and had often threatened to destroy the child to be revenged on her husband. That when she was tried for strangling a woman through jealousy, it would have gone very hard against her, had not Mr Jaggers been on her side, and that he had worked the case up so cleverly that he was too many for the jury, and the woman was acquitted.

"She went into his service directly after her acquittal," added Wemmick, "tamed as you see her now."

"Was the child a boy or a girl?" asked Pip.

And Wemmick answered, "Said to be a girl."

They parted then, and Pip went home with strange thoughts, and the day after he went to see Miss Havisham.

There was an air of such utter loneliness upon her that Pip felt full of pity. "Mr Jaggers gave me your note yesterday," he said. "And I have lost no time."

Then she told him to tell her from the beginning about that partnership for Herbert. And after Pip had told her all she said:

"If I give you the nine hundred pounds for this purpose, will you keep my secret as you have kept your own?"

"Quite as faithfully," answered Pip.

She took from her pocket a yellow set of ivory tablets, and wrote upon them with a pencil in a case of tarnished gold. "Give that to Mr Jaggers," she said. "And he will let you have the money."

Her hand trembled as she gave him the tablets. And then she said, "My name is on the flyleaf. If you can ever write under my name, 'I forgive her,' pray do it."

"Oh, Miss Havisham!" cried Pip, "I can do it now. There have been sore mistakes. And I want forgiveness far too much to be bitter with you."

Then to Pip's amazement, she burst into tears. "Oh!" she cried despairingly, "What have I done! What have I done!"

Pip knew not how to answer, or how to comfort her. But after a while she grew more composed. "Is Estella married?" he said.

She answered, "Yes."

"Miss Havisham, may I ask you a question about Estella? Whose child was she?"

"I do not know," she said. "Mr Jaggers brought her here. I told him that I wanted a little girl to rear and love. And one night he brought her here asleep, and I called her Estella."

"Might I ask her age then."

"Two or three."

Pip left her. Twilight was closing in, and he took a walk round the ruined garden for the last time—round by the paths where he and Estella had walked. Oh! How lonely and dreary it all was!

Then he returned to the house, went upstairs to say goodbye, and saw Miss Havisham seated in a chair upon the hearth close to the fire. At the same moment he saw a great flaming light spring up, and she was running at him, shrieking, with a whirl of fire playing all about her.

Pip had a double greatcoat on, and flinging it off, he closed with her, threw her down, and got it over her.

Then he dragged the great cloth from the table, for the same purpose, and with it dragged down the rotten bride-cake in the midst; and while the disturbed beetles and spiders ran away over the floor, he held her down with all his strength until the flames were out.

Her faded bridal dress was burnt to ashes, and she was insensible, and Pip was afraid to have her moved. But a surgeon soon arrived, and, by his orders, her bed was carried into the room, and laid upon the great table, and there her injuries were dressed.

Pip was astonished to see that both his hands were burnt, and his left arm was also burnt to the elbow; but he arranged to carry the news to Mr Pocket, and left for London by the early morning coach.

His burns had been dressed by the surgeon before he left, and after Herbert had taken the news to his father, he returned to their chambers and devoted the day to attending to Pip, taking the bandages off his hands, to steep them in cooling liquid, and putting them on again.

"Handel," he said, "I sat with Provis two good hours last night. Do you know he improves very much?"

"I told you I thought he was softened," answered Pip.

"So you did. He told me much of his life," went on Herbert, "and about his wife—a jealous woman, and a revengeful woman, who was tried for murder, but who was acquitted through the cleverness of Mr Jaggers—My dear Handel, I have hurt you. Was I rough?"

"It is impossible to be gentler, Herbert. Tell me every word," said Pip. And his heart beat fast.

"They had a child—a little girl of whom Provis was very fond, and on the very evening of the murder, she swore that she would destroy the child, and that he would never see it again. Then she vanished—Are you in pain, dear fellow? You seem to breathe quickly."

"Herbert, did the woman keep her oath?"

"She did. And though he grieved greatly for the child, he kept himself dark, as he says, out of the way of the trial, lest he should be called upon to bear witness that she had killed the child. After the acquittal she disappeared, and thus he lost both child and wife."

"Herbert, look at me," said Pip. 'You are not afraid that my senses are wandering from the accident of last night?"

"You are rather excited, Handel," said Herbert. "But you are quite yourself."

"I know I am quite myself," answered Pip. "Herbert, the man we have in hiding down the river is *Estella's father!*"

14

Flight

Pip's left arm took so long to heal, that he was still unable to get a coat on. But while Herbert was away in the City, Pip sent for Clarriker to come to him, and he had the great satisfaction of completing the business of the partnership.

Clarriker told him that the affairs of the house were steadily progressing, that he would now be able to establish a small branch house in Cairo, the capital of Egypt, and that Herbert, as the new partner, would go out and take charge of it.

So that matter was settled, and Pip felt it was the only good thing he had done since he had first heard of his great expectations.

And now, on a Monday morning, when Pip and Herbert were at breakfast, the signal came from Wemmick. It was in a short letter of a few lines:

"WALWORTH.—*Burn this as soon as read. On Wednesday you might do what you know of, if you felt disposed to try it. Now burn.*"

When Pip had shown this to Herbert, and had put it into the fire, they considered what to do, for Pip's arm was still too painful to pull an oar.

"Faithful dear boy, well done!"

"I know a better course than taking a Thames waterman," said Herbert. "Take Startop. He is a good fellow, a skilled hand, and fond of us."

"But how much would you tell him, Herbert?"

"I would tell him there is urgent reason for getting Provis aboard and away. Nothing more."

It was arranged, then, that Provis should be got down the river in a boat, well beyond Gravesend, and lie by there till a foreign steamer came down from London.

Herbert went off directly to make inquiries, and learned that a steamer for Hamburg, in Germany, would start from London, at about nine on Thursday morning. Then he went off to Startop's lodgings.

Startop was more than ready to join, and they settled that he and Herbert would pull a pair of oars, Pip would steer, and Provis would be sitter and keep quiet.

Herbert, then, went to Mill-Pond Bank, and prepared Provis to come down to some stairs hard by the house on Wednesday morning, as soon as he saw the boat approach.

Where Pip might go with the convict, what he might do, or when he might return, were questions utterly unknown to him. His mind was wholly set on Provis's safety. And when Wednesday morning dawned, he took with him nothing but a few necessaries in a bag.

Pip and Startop loitered down to the Temple stairs. Herbert followed, and by half-past eight they were off. Pip felt mortified to be of so little use in the boat; but there were few better oarsmen than his two friends, and they rowed with a steady stroke.

Barges, sailing colliers, and coasting traders were dropping down with the tide; and among many skiffs and wherries, their boat went ahead briskly. Old London Bridge was soon passed, and old Billingsgate Market. Then they passed the White Tower and the Traitor's Gate, and were in among the tiers of shipping. Here at her moorings, was tomorrow's steamer for Hamburg. And now Pip, sitting in the stern, could see, with a faster-beating heart, Mill-Pond stairs.

"Is he there?" said Herbert.

"Not yet," answered Pip.

"Right! He was not to come down till he saw us."

"I see him now!" said Pip. "Pull both. Easy, Herbert. Oars."

They touched the stairs lightly for a single moment, the convict was on board, and they were off again. He had a boat cloak with him, and a black canvas bag, and looked just like a river pilot.

"Dear boy!" he said, putting his arm on Pip's shoulder, as he took his seat. "Faithful dear boy, well done! Thank'ee, thank'ee."

As they had taken him aboard, Pip had looked warily around for any token of their being suspected, but he had seen none. Certainly no boat attended or followed them.

"If you knowed, dear boy," whispered Provis, "what it is to sit here alonger my dear boy, and have my smoke, arter having been day by day betwixt four walls, you'd envy me."

"If all goes well," said Pip, "you will be perfectly free and safe again within a few hours."

"Dear boy," he said, "we can no more see to the bottom of the next few hours, than we can see to the bottom of this river."

"You are not despondent?" asked Pip.

"Not a bit of it, dear boy." And putting his black pipe into his mouth, with an undisturbed expression of face, he sat as contented as if he were already out of England. Indeed, he was the least anxious of any of them, and said he hoped to live to see his gentleman one of the best gentlemen in a foreign country.

The air felt cold upon the river, but it was a bright day, and the sunshine was very cheering, and the tide was yet with them when they were off Gravesend. But after that the tide began to slacken, and they kept under shore, standing carefully off from low shallows and mud banks.

Then they got ashore, ate and drank what they had brought with them, and looked about. After that they pushed off again, but it was harder work now. Herbert and Startop, however, persevered, and rowed and rowed until the sun went down.

As the night was now falling fast, they made up their minds to lie by at the first lonely tavern they could find. So, plying their oars, and speaking little, they held on for four or five miles.

And now, for the first time, they were possessed with the idea that they were followed, and one would say in a low voice, "What was that ripple?" Or another, "Is that a boat yonder?"

At last they saw a light and a roof, and ran alongside a little causeway made of stones.

Leaving the rest in the boat, Pip stepped ashore and found the light to be in the window of a public house. And here he engaged two double-bedded rooms.

Then they all came ashore, hauling the boat up for the night, and made a very good meal by the kitchen fire.

No other company was in the house than the landlord, his wife, and a grizzled old sailor. And while they were comforting themselves by the fire after their supper, the sailor asked Pip if they had seen a four-oared galley going up with the tide.

"No," said Pip.

"They must ha' thought better on't for some reason or other then," said the sailor, "and gone down."

"A four-oared galley, did you say?" said Pip.

"A four," answered the sailor, "and two sitters."

"You thinks they was Custom 'Us, eh, Jack?" said the landlord.

"I do," said the sailor. "A four and two sitters don't go hovering up with the tide and down with another, without their being Custom 'Us at the bottom of it."

This conversation made the guests very uneasy, for a four-oared galley, hovering about in so unusual a way, was an ugly circumstance.

On going to bed, Pip lay down with the greater part of his clothes on, and slept well for a few hours. Rising softly then, for the convict lay fast asleep, Pip looked out of the window and saw, by the light of the clouded moon, that two men were looking into their boat.

His first impulse was to call up Herbert, but on his way to the other bedroom, he remembered that Herbert and Startop had had a hard day and must be greatly fatigued, and he went back to his own room.

Going to the window, he saw the two men walking away, and feeling very cold, he lay down and fell asleep again.

They were up early. And Pip thought it right to tell what he had seen. Again the convict was the least anxious of the party.

"The men belonged to the Custom 'Us, most likely," he said. "They had no thought of us, dear boy."

However, Pip proposed that after breakfast he and Provis should walk together to a distant point, and that the boat should take them aboard there.

All agreed. And Pip and Provis started off, reaching the point about twelve o'clock, and there they waited until they saw the boat coming round.

Getting aboard, they rowed out into the track of the expected steamer, and began to look out for her smoke But it was half-past one before they saw her smoke; and as she was coming on at full speed, they said goodbye to Herbert and Startop.

And neither Herbert's eyes nor Pip's were quite dry, when Pip saw a four-oared galley shoot out from under the bank but a little way ahead of them, and row out into the same track.

The steamer was coming on fast, and Pip, calling to Herbert to keep before the tide, that she might see them lying by for her, cautioned Provis to sit quite still and keep his cloak about him.

"Dear boy, trust to me," answered the convict.

Meantime the galley, which was skilfully handled, had crossed them, let them come up with her, and fallen alongside; drifting when they drifted, and pulling a stroke or two when they pulled.

Of the two sitters, one held the rudder lines, and looked at them attentively—as did all the rowers. The other sitter was wrapped up, much as Provis was, and seemed to shrink and whisper something to the steerer as he looked at them. But not a word was spoken in either boat.

The steamer was nearing them very fast, and the beating of her paddles grew louder and louder. And at that moment the galley hailed them.

"You have a returned convict there," cried the man who held the lines. "That's the man, wrapped in the cloak. His name is Abel Magwitch, otherwise Provis. I apprehend that man, and call upon him to surrender." And running the galley aboard of them, they were holding on to their gunwale, before those in the boat knew what they were doing.

This caused great confusion on board the steamer, and Pip heard them calling to them; while an order was shouted to stop her paddles.

In the same moment the steersman of the galley laid his hand on Magwitch's shoulder, while Magwitch, starting up and leaning across the steersman, pulled the cloak from the neck of the shrinking sitter in the galley, and Pip saw that the face disclosed was the face of the other convict of long ago—Compeyson.

He saw the face tilt back with a white terror on it, and heard a great cry on board the steamer, and a loud splash in the water, and felt the boat sink from under him.

It was but for an instant that Pip seemed to struggle in the water, and then he was taken on board the galley. Herbert was there, and Startop was there; but their boat was gone, and the two convicts were gone too.

The steamer was furiously blowing off her steam, but the crew of the galley righted her with great speed, and pulling certain swift, strong strokes ahead, lay upon their oars, every man looking eagerly at the water for the two convicts.

Presently a dark object was seen in it, bearing towards them on the tide. And Pip saw that it was Magwitch swimming, but that he was swimming very feebly indeed.

He was taken on board, and irons were put on his ankles and wrists. And the galley being kept steady, they watched the water again for Compeyson.

By this time the steamer was drifting away from them, and still no Compeyson had appeared. Everybody knew that it was hopeless now to look for him, and slowly they pulled away.

15

All Over

Magwitch—Provis no longer—had received some severe injury to the chest and head. He told Pip that he believed himself to have gone under the keel of the steamer, and to have been struck as he rose again.

He whispered, that as he had laid his hand on Compeyson's cloak to identify him, the villain had staggered back, and they had both gone overboard together. That they had gone down, fiercely locked in each other's arms, and that there had been a struggle in the water.

What he had done to Compeyson, Magwitch did not say; only that he, disengaging himself, had struck out and swam away.

The officer, who steered the galley, took charge of everything the prisoner had about him; and the thick pocketbook passed into his hands. He gave Pip leave to accompany Magwitch to London; but Herbert and Startop he put ashore.

Pip did not shudder from Magwitch now, and in the hunted creature, who held his hand in his, he only saw a man who had meant to be his benefactor, and who had thought of him affectionately for many years.

Magwitch had been severely injured, and Pip often heard him groan.

"How grieved I am," said Pip, compassionately, "to think you came back for my sake."

"Dear boy," he said, "I'm quite content to take my chance. I've seen my boy, and he can be a gentleman without me."

But Pip knew—though he did not tell him so—that should Magwitch be convicted, his possessions would be forfeited to the Crown.

He was taken to the police court next day; and an old officer of the prison ship from which he had escaped to the marshes, came to identify him.

Compeyson had hoped to do that; but Compeyson was dead, and his body was tumbling on the tides.

Magwitch was committed to take his trial at the next Sessions. And the next Sessions—or term when a court meets for business—would come on in a month's time.

He lay in the prison infirmary, very ill, for he had broken two ribs and injured one of his lungs, and breathed with great difficulty and pain. But the fact of his being in the infirmary, and not in the common prison, gave Pip the opportunity of seeing him every day.

It was at this dark time of Pip's life that Herbert returned home one evening, a good deal cast down "My dear Handel," he said, "I fear I shall soon have to leave you. I am going to Cairo. Handel, have you thought about your future?"

"No," said Pip, "for I have been afraid to think of my future."

"In this branch house of ours, Handel, we must have a—" And, in his delicacy, Herbert hesitated.

"A clerk," put in Pip.

"A clerk," repeated Herbert. "Dear fellow, will you come to me?"

"Give me two or three months before I decide," pleaded Pip. For it was impossible, he knew, to leave Magwitch at present.

Herbert agreed. And at the end of the week he left for Cairo in high hope.

Pip visited Magwitch every day, and every day the prisoner became worse and weaker. Then the Sessions came round, and though Mr Jaggers asked that the trial should be postponed, his application was not granted.

So the trial came on at once, and when Magwitch was put to the bar, he was seated in a chair. No objection was made to Pip's sitting close to the dock, on the outside of it, and holding the hand that the convict stretched forth to him.

The trial was very short, and the jury finding him guilty, the judge sentenced Magwitch to be hanged.

"My lord," said the prisoner, rising for a moment, "I have received my sentence of death from the Almighty, but I bow to yours."

Then he had to be helped from his chair, and to go very slowly, holding Pip's hand all the while.

Pip prayed that he might die before the sentence could be carried out; and as the days went on, thanked God that the convict was getting weaker.

On the tenth day, his eyes were turned towards the door, and lighted up as Pip entered, and Pip saw that a greater change had come.

"Dear boy," he said, as Pip sat down by the bed, "I thought you was late. But I knowed you couldn't be that."

"It is just the time," said Pip. "I waited for it at the gate."

"You always waits at the gate, don't you, dear boy?" he said.

"Yes. Not to lose a moment of the time."

"God bless you. You've never deserted me, dear boy!"

Pip pressed his hand. And Magwitch, smiling, signed to him to lay his hand upon his breast. Pip laid it there, and smiling again, the convict put both his hands upon it.

While they sat thus, the allotted time ran out; but looking round, Pip found the governor of the prison standing near. He whispered, "You needn't go yet."

Pip thanked him, gratefully. And the governor, stepping aside, beckoned the officer away, for he saw that the end was come.

"Dear Magwitch, I must tell you now," whispered Pip. "You understand what I say?"

He gently pressed Pip's hand.

"You had a child once, whom you loved and lost."

Again he pressed his hand.

"She lived, and found powerful friends. She is a lady, and very beautiful. And I love her."

With a last faint effort, he raised Pip's hand to his lips, and passed away, and his head dropped quietly on his breast.

Pip got ill after that—ill of a wasting fever. He had scarcely any money now, and two men came to arrest him for debt; but, fearing that his sickness might be catching, they left the chambers, and Pip lay unconscious and very ill.

For a long while he lay unconscious. Then he began to dream of Joe, and when his senses came back to him at last, he saw that the face bending over him so tenderly was really Joe's.

"Is it Joe?" he said.

And the dear old home voice answered, "Which it air, old chap."

"Oh, Joe, you break my heart," said Pip. "Look angry at me, Joe. Tell me of my ingratitude."

But Joe replied, "You and me was ever friends, Pip." And put his head down on the pillow at Pip's side.

Pip got better after that, and Joe told him all the home news. And told him, too, that Miss Havisham was dead, and that she had left all her money to Estella.

He knew, too, who Pip's benefactor had been, but they did not talk much of that, nor upon the fact that Pip's great expectations were all gone.

Then one morning when Pip was well, he found that Joe had left the chambers, leaving this short letter on the breakfast table:—

"Not wishful to intrude I have departured fur you are well again, dear Pip and will do better without JO."

"P.S.—Ever the best of friends."

And enclosed in the letter was a receipt for the debt on which Pip had been arrested, and which Joe had paid out of his own savings.

Three days after, Pip followed him to the old village, but there was no clink of Joe's hammer as he approached the forge. And when he reached it, the place was shut up and still.

But the house was not deserted, and going softly towards it, and peeping through the window, he saw Joe and Biddy standing together arm-in-arm.

In another moment Biddy had rushed out, and had flung her arms round Pip's neck.

"Why, dear Biddy, how smart you are!" said Pip.

And Biddy cried, in a burst of happiness, "It is my wedding day, and I am married to Joe!"

Pip sold all he had, and went out to Cairo and joined Herbert. But many a year went round before he became a partner in the House.

He heard of Estella leading a most unhappy life, and then he heard of the death of her husband.

For eleven years he had not seen Joe nor Biddy though he had álways written regularly to them; and then upon an afternoon in December, he found himself again at the old forge.

He turned the handle of the door so softly that he was not heard, and there, smoking his pipe in the old place by the kitchen firelight, sat Joe. And there, fenced into Pip's old corner, with Joe's leg, and sitting on Pip's own little stool, was Joe's little son.

"We giv' him the name of Pip for your sake, dear old chap," said Joe.

And Biddy came to welcome him with a little girl in her arms.

That same evening Pip found his way to Miss Havisham's old place; but no house was standing there now—nothing but the wall of the old garden. A gate in the fence was standing ajar, and pushing it open, he went in.

The evening was not dark, and the moon was rising, and as Pip went along the desolate garden walk, he beheld a solitary figure in it.

The figure stopped, as if much surprised, and quickly uttered his name. And Pip cried out, "Estella!"

It was Estella, indeed. "I am greatly changed," she said. "I wonder you know me."

The freshness of her beauty was gone, but its indescribable charm remained. Like Pip, she, too, had come to look at the old place, and she told him that the ground was now going to be built upon, and she had come to take leave of it before its change.

"I have often thought of you," said Estella

And Pip said, "You have always held your place in *my* heart."

Then they were silent. And Pip, taking her hand in his, led her out of the ruined garden.

And as they went, Estella told him that suffering had bent and broken her. "I hope," she added, "into a better shape."

And Pip, still holding her hand in his, knew that Estella loved him at last, and that there was no need for them to part again.